SERGEANT CLUFF
GOES FISHING

Detective-Sergeant Cluff is at home in the bleak, moorland market town of 1960s Gunnarshaw. A gruff and gloomy loner, he has spent a lifetime observing local folk – and knows their lives inside out. They know him, too – a bulky, macintoshed figure who watches from the shadows of Gunnarshaw's ginnels as they go about their daily business, his dog Clive always at his side.

But it's not just criminals Cluff has to watch out for. Never satisfied with easy answers to cases, Cluff is a maverick and no flatterer to authority – much to the bemusement of Detective-Constable Barker, but much more so to the despair of the hapless Inspector Mole, who tries at every opportunity to outwit or contain Cluff's singular methods of detection.

But beneath Cluff's dour exterior beats the heart of a truly compassionate man who possesses a deep understanding of human nature, in all its sordid and depraved details – details which frequently push Cluff to bend the rules in his pursuit of moral justice.

Gil North's novels, which follow the investigations of Detective-Sergeant Cluff in the fictional and close-knit moorland market town of Gunnarshaw, were first published in the 1960s. Incredibly popular, they were adapted for BBC Television and regularly attracted twelve million viewers. Gil North wrote the scripts for every episode.

Gil North was the pen-name of Geoffrey Horne (1916–1988). He was born in Skipton, North Yorkshire, where his father was Town Clerk. Horne was educated at the local grammar school, then studied at Christ's College, Cambridge, before embarking on a career as a civil servant in Nigeria and Cameroon.

He later returned to pursue his writing ambitions in his native Skipton, which was not only the inspiration for Gunnarshaw, but also the location where the television drama *Cluff* was filmed.

SERGEANT CLUFF GOES FISHING

Gil North

GREAT NORTHERN

This edition published 2021 by
Great Northern Books
PO Box 1380, Bradford,
West Yorkshire, BD5 5FB

www.greatnorthernbooks.co.uk

© Gil North Limited 2021

Originally published in 1962 by Chapman & Hall Ltd

ISBN: 978-1-912101-42-9

Design by David Burrill

CIP Data
A catalogue for this book is available from the British Library

CHAPTER I

"Give me those!"

Betty Metcalfe started: "You frightened me—"

Anthea Ambler snatched the letters from the maid and sorted them rapidly, extracting an envelope, thrusting it unopened into the pocket of her mackintosh. She held out the rest: "Take them to the Colonel."

She stayed where she was and she could hear the feet of Sam Rycroft, in his capacity as postman, retreating down the drive to the main gate, returning to his shop-cum-post-office. She watched Betty into a passage alongside the staircase, Betty disappearing into the library. She was still there when Betty came out. The maid's eyes met hers and the maid swung away, going farther along the passage to the kitchen.

Her father's voice called, "Anthea!"

"I'm here."

"The flowers—?"

"I'm just going."

She waited and the house was quiet. After a while she opened the closed front door and stepped on to the porch, shutting the door behind her. She took the letter from her pocket and slit the envelope with her thumbnail. She glanced at the contents of the envelope. A smile played for a moment about her bloodless lips, which were innocent of make-up. The smile vanished as quickly as it had appeared.

She walked in front of the house, between it and the lawns, to the flower-gardens and the greenhouses. A pimply youth peered from a potting-shed, his face insolent, matching his manner. She looked at him questioningly and he said, "In a minute."

Walt Sims backed into the shed, languidly, not hurrying. She could see him, purposely slow, winding raffia round freshly-cut stalks. When he was ready he offered her a large bunch of chrysanthemums, their blooms bronze and yellow.

The village was grey in the light of the late-September morning. Beyond the church, beyond the Rectory next to the church, low, grey cottages grew from the land, one with the land, interspersed by larger farm-houses, flanked by their barns and outbuildings. The cottages and the farms ribboned the road and a half-mile or so ahead of her the road bent sharply, a shop at the corner facing her down its length.

Josh Lambert touched the brim of his helmet with his hand. He said, "Miss Ambler," straight-faced, a little surlily, and she returned his greeting in a perfunctory fashion, "Constable." She went through the lych-gate into the churchyard and the constable strolled in her wake. The constable halted in the shelter of the gate, under the roof of the gate, his back to the road. High fells encircled the village, their lower slopes netted with a mesh of white stone walls, the open wilds above the walls patched brown with dying bracken. The wind blew keenly from the tops of the fells and the gate protected the constable from its edge.

Gravestones, weathered and leaning, faced each other across the narrow gravel path. The church rose greyer than the houses of the village, squat, its square tower stubby, very old.

Its door creaked, and creaked again. Lambert put a hand like a ham to his beefy face and scratched his chin. He wondered how much the flowers for the church resulted from her own inclination, how much from the Colonel's conception of his duty to the village.

Somewhere in the distance a tractor chugged, the sound of it mingling with the murmur of the river. A peewit swooped, screaming, over a field up the road. A private path led from the Hall to the church, through the wall separating the grounds of the Hall and the churchyard, and if she'd wanted to she could have taken the path. The Rectory on the other side of the church had its own access too, by a path the twin of the first.

The constable backed closer to the cold stones walling the gate. His features remained wooden, expressionless. The uneven strands of his heavy moustache overhung his thick upper lip. His cheeks were rough, pickled red by his years in the dale. The dark blue of his uniform toned with the darkness of his background, making him inconspicuous in spite of his size. His eyes tracked the Rector, almost running between the graves. He nodded to himself, feeling a momentary twinge of satisfaction.

She stopped in the nave, listening to the quick steps on the flagged floor, past the font, along the aisle behind her. The Rector's thin, transparent hands reached to relieve her of the flowers and she clung to the flowers. The Rector sighed. The Rector asked, "How is he today?"

"As usual," she replied.

Tall and spare, a beanpole of a man, Canon Staveley stumbled for the vestry, untidy, a rusty, food-spotted cassock flapping about his ankles. Water flowed noisily from a tap.

Water flopped over the rims of the vases he was carrying to her, splashing at his feet. By the altar she said, "That one," and "That one." He handed to her obediently the stems she indicated.

The walls of the church climbed into shadowy recesses amongst a great web of oak beams. Sculptured, recumbent figures lay supine on the tops of tombs in the chancel. Here and there brass memorial-tablets glimmered faintly. A draught stirred the tattered cloth of a banner on a staff by the stained-glass window.

The Rector said, "Anthea—"

She bent to retrieve a fragment of petal from the choir steps. Older than she was but not greatly older, in his fifties, he was at her heels when she left the church, and this time she took the shorter way to the Hall, as if she was eager to be rid of him. The words he'd been going to say died on his lips. He saw less and less of her and he wanted to see more and more. He stared at the Hall, visible through the branches of the trees. Falling leaves drifted gently about him. His eyelids drooped over his sad, faithful eyes and his heart twisted.

Back at the house she leaned over her father's chair. Her father's head rested against the chair-back and purple tinted his once florid features, patterned with a network of capillaries. His hands lay weightless on the padded, leather arms of the chair, more transparent than the Rector's, their skin like parchment. The Colonel's knees pointed the cloth of his trousers, all of him bony, hardly anything of him left except bone and sinew, his flesh melted away.

"You'll lunch in here?" she said.

The Colonel protested, weakly, "You treat me like an

invalid."

"I'll tell Betty to bring it in."

"I'm not ill."

"Exertion's bad for you."

She added, "I have to go into Gunnarshaw. Is there anything you want?"

The Colonel began, "I'm surrounded by women—" He said, "Haven't you heard from Robert?"

"Not for a while."

"Can't he come more often?"

"He has his own affairs to attend to."

She avoided the arm that was groping for her. She said, "What is it?"

He told her, "After all, what difference will it make? I think sometimes—"

"Yes?"

"I've seen so little of him. What I have seen—"

"Isn't your mind made up?"

"It's not too late."

She said, "You forget, I'm not a man," her tone faintly bitter, and he didn't hear her, his gaze riveted upon a photograph, in a silver frame, on an occasional table between his chair and the fireplace.

A youngish man, not unlike the Colonel, in the uniform of a gunner officer, stared back sightlessly from the frame.

CHAPTER II

They said in Gunnarshaw that the High Street was Cluff's office. The Sergeant leaned on his stick in the High Street, almost as permanent in the street as the parish church at its top or the statue in front of the public library.

The rain began at noon. It blackened the shoulders of his Burberry and made limper the limp brim of his tweed hat. It dripped from the branches of the trees planted at intervals in the setts by the kerbs and shone blackly on the macadamed road, streaming along the gutters to disappear through the gratings of drains. The Sergeant ignored the rain. He forgot what time it was. He watched the street, without seeming to watch the street, not consciously aware that he was watching the street, unable, if he had been asked, to say why he was watching it. His dog squatted beside him, as still as himself. Rain filmed his red cheeks and beaded the dog's long, moisture-flattened fur.

She drove the car competently on to the setts some distance from where the Sergeant stood, parking the car with its bonnet aiming at the shops. She got out of the car, locking its door, not much shorter than the Colonel but more slender than Cluff liked a woman to be, her breasts immature, her hips narrow. The Sergeant, if she noticed him, failed to register with her and she walked fast, purposefully, away from him. His brow creased and he frowned.

He clicked his tongue at the dog in a curt sound of command. A loose flag sank under his weight, spurting a tiny spray of water from the crack between it and its neighbour, squelching back into its bed as he trod it down. His stick swung in time with his strides, its ferrule tapping, towards the short flight of steps she'd descended. A glass-panelled door at the bottom of the steps opened into a semi-basement. Beyond the steps the sill of a window, lace curtaining its panes, lifted hardly higher than the level of the road.

He angled out on to the setts, to get a better view inside the café. Anthea Ambler sat at a round table on one side of a fireplace which had crêpe paper crinkled in its hearth instead of a fire, her back so foursquarely to the window that the Sergeant suspected her position deliberately arranged. Her arm extended, offering her companion a cup, and she had been so short a time in the café that the order must have been placed before her arrival, ready and waiting for her.

The Sergeant stared, unabashed, careless whether or not anyone in the street noted his curiosity. He thought back and he'd seen the man who took the cup before, not often, once or twice, not staying in Gunnarshaw, driving past Cluff on the pavement. The man's hands fluttered in emphasis of the points his lips were making and his city glitter, his urban smoothness, attracted the Sergeant no more than on former occasions. Her plainness and country aspect contrasted with the man's smartness and they were queerly assorted, she the elder but not so much the elder that she could have been mistaken for his mother or as like him as a sister. The Sergeant put a name to the man, with no more justification than his knowledge of what went on in the dales, gleaned in the High Street from the farmers who came in on market days. He didn't doubt his identification. He wasn't in the habit of admitting himself in the wrong.

The minutes passed and the rain continued, forming a mist that shrouded the moors above the town, diaphanous about the moor-tops. The Sergeant stirred. He made for the entrance to a ginnel that burrowed through the buildings on that side of the High Street and expanded behind into a scarcely wider cobbled footway separating rows of cottage-houses. He stopped in the mouth of the ginnel, out of sight of passers-by unless they were crossing directly in front of the opening. He gestured his dog to him.

The clock in the church tower struck a half-hour and then the three-quarters. It began the hour and Sergeant Cluff, stolid, calm, counted the strokes, automatically, without interest, content so long as her car stayed there, across the pavement opposite to him.

The car started. The car backed. She was alone in the car as she had been when she arrived in Gunnarshaw. He waited until the car had driven away before leaving the ginnel, his dog disciplined without so much as a glance. He looked both ways along the street, the street and its people familiar to him, only the man she'd taken tea with foreign.

The Sergeant set himself into ponderous movement, Clive beside him, his shoulders hunched about his bull-neck, big-bellied. The man from the café went jauntily in front, self-satisfied, surrounded by an aura of contempt for Gunnarshaw, nothing in Gunnarshaw to disturb him, the inhabitants of Gunnarshaw equally of no account.

They reached the bottom of the High Street, one man behind the other, Robert Todd ahead, unrealizing, Sergeant Caleb Cluff in the rear, unthinking, not allowing himself to think. They turned right at the post office and crossed the bridge over the canal. A mill climbed skyward on one side of them and on the other engines coughed and wagons clashed in a shunting-yard. The dog padded softly and the dog's master made no more noise than the dog.

The booking-clerk at the railway station stared through his pigeon-hole at the Sergeant. He saw rather than heard the Sergeant murmuring to his dog, Clive sitting patiently on the wooden floor of the booking-hall. A Diesel train whistled, loudly, lengthily, mournfully, its wheels beginning to grate on the lines. The Sergeant passed the ticket-collector in his box by the barrier to the platform, and the collector said, "Caleb."

The track wound to the south, following the floor of the valley, worming between the hills. The rear unit of the Diesel threaded a maze of rails, picking up speed, getting smaller and smaller. Cluff scowled after it. A steam-train, coming from the direction in which the Diesel was going, rushed through the station without stopping, discarded wrappings on the opposite platform fluttering. The passengers in the express glanced from their compartments in a superior manner, Gunnarshaw to them only a wayside halt too unimportant to merit their attention. White-coated attendants moved amongst the tables in a restaurant car. The engine howled, its howls snapping the signals into position for miles to the north, like guardsmen.

"A single ticket?" Cluff demanded.

The collector told him, "The other half of a day-return."

"Second-class?"

"First."

"Naturally."

"I was on duty when he got here," the collector volunteered.

"How long since?"

"A couple of hours." The collector fiddled with a ticket-punch. "People like that usually have cars."

"A train's less noticeable."

"What for?"

"You've seen him in the station before?"

The collector replied, "Not when I've been about." He was going to ask, "What's he done?" but Cluff and the dog were half-way across the booking-hall already.

The collector called out instead, "It's been quiet for you this year—"

He didn't expect a reply and he didn't get one.

CHAPTER III

The Sergeant ambled to the High Street, shadowed by Clive. The wind, with more than a touch of autumn in it, played with the leaves falling from the trees, chasing them along the pavements. The windows of the shops blazed with lights, the evenings drawing in, the sodden summer a memory. He slowed and then his pace quickened again. The people he met nodded their heads and he ignored them. They left him alone but little flickers of interest ran across their faces. They looked at each other knowingly, wisely, and allowed their eyes to wander to the Sergeant and back from the Sergeant, their own consciences clear.

The Sergeant turned the corner by the church. He passed the houses on the hill, Gunnarshaw's residential quarter. The houses ended and hawthorn berries festooned the hedges on either side of him in red clusters. The larger spheres of rose-hips showed redder than the hawthorns. On the fruiting brambles the blackberries were still green. Cattle peered at him from the fields, their flanks caked with mud. Ewes bleated at lambs grown, since the spring, as big as themselves.

His feet rustled the leaves in the lane branching from the road to his cottage, treading the spiked cases under the horse-chestnuts. He opened the door of the cottage with the key he took from beneath a flat stone in an empty flowerbed by the

porch, surprised that he'd reached the cottage. He closed the
door behind him and hung his Burberry and his hat on a peg
in the passage, leaning his stick in a corner.

He went into the living-room. His cat, Jenet, in a chair by
the fire, winked an eye, pretending not to see him. The fire
burnt cheerfully, made up by Annie Croft, who came in the
mornings to clean the cottage. The Sergeant poked the fire,
alone in the house at this time of day except for his dog and
his cat, but no more alone than he'd been since leaving the
railway station. He put an elbow on the mantelpiece, staring
into the fire, uneasy, the cause of his uneasiness a vagueness
in his mind on which he couldn't put a finger. Clive moved
quietly, pleading with the Sergeant, but gently. The cat slept.

Cluff collected himself. He fed the dog and, because the
dog was eating, he ate too. Afterwards he took the dog outside
and relocked the door, replacing the key under the stone. The
dog preceded him to the car in the shed against the gable of
the cottage. The dog gazed at him from the car seat, through
the yellowed windscreen, as he swung the starting-handle. He
managed to get the car going and drove off erratically. The
ancient bull-nosed Morris ground and rattled, shooting gases
from its cracked exhaust in a series of explosions.

He drove for half an hour, not to Egilsby where the Colonel
lived, where the woman in the café lived with the Colonel,
but to a village in the same direction, larger than Egilsby, too
small to ape Gunnarshaw's claim to the dignity of a township.
The driver of a red single-decked bus pulled in close to the
side of the narrow road and waved as the Sergeant went
by, both the Sergeant and the Sergeant's car unmistakable,
the Sergeant upright behind the steering-wheel, tense with

concentration, his eyes fixed on the road, the dog with its head on top of the door, nose into the wind. The limestone walls unravelled and the road dipped and climbed, each rise steeper than the last. He stopped finally in a cobbled market place with a stone cross and cottages about it, and a few shops and three public-houses. He switched off his engine. The plume of steam escaping from his radiator-cap died away. He looked at his watch and continued to sit in the car.

The small, slow procession of men and women coming out of the house the Sergeant was watching dried up. He left the dog in the car. He went into a waiting-room, with benches round its walls and a table in the middle of the floor. Copies of magazines, dog-eared and tattered, littered the table. A last patient from the surgery glanced inquiringly at him. A voice shouted, "Any more?"

The owner of the voice looked up from the card on which he was writing. The voice exclaimed, "Good God!" and the doctor sat back, middle-aged, red-faced, in tweeds as disreputable as the Sergeant's. He put his pen down: "I don't flatter myself you're here for my professional advice."

"It's not as bad as that."

"I haven't forgotten Thistlethwaite at Ghyll End last year."*

"I hoped you'd remember."

The doctor's eyes narrowed and his expression was shrewd.

"You weren't involved," Cluff added.

"My colleague was. Round these parts they haven't the faith in medicos they once had." The doctor got to his feet. "Who's dead I ought to have kept alive?"

* *The Methods of Sergeant Cluff*

"No one."

"That's not the relief it should be," Doctor Forsythe said. He twisted the handle of a door behind his desk. "At least you can let me down in comfort."

The doctor swirled whisky in his glass. Cluff smelt his drink. He rolled it in his mouth, savouring it. The doctor murmured, "My Hippocratic oath?" dryly facetious.

"You know me," Cluff said.

The doctor answered the question Cluff had asked. "I can't deny it, can I? The Colonel's my patient."

The Sergeant waited.

"I call at the Hall sometimes," Forsythe said.

"Often?"

"How many villages have I got to look after?" The doctor sipped his whisky. "The Colonel's old enough to be your father, or mine."

"If you stretch a point."

"He's well looked after."

"How well?"

The doctor's eyebrows lifted. He stared at the bottom of his glass. He said, "Very well."

"She deserves credit."

"Miss Ambler? What other interest has she left?" The doctor emptied his glass. He sounded slightly worried. He reached for the decanter and jabbed it at Cluff. He asked, "What is it about you that puts the wind up a man?"

Cluff tipped the decanter: "It's a pity she couldn't have been a son too."

The doctor said, "The Colonel's over seventy. At that age the heart's not as strong as it was, nor the arteries as supple."

"He could die at any time?"

"Couldn't you? Couldn't I?"

"Or live for years?"

"I wouldn't put it as high as that."

The Sergeant climbed to his feet: "I shouldn't have troubled you."

"Don't you go to the Hall these days?"

"Isn't the nephew there on occasions?"

"Todd won't bite you."

"The Colonel doesn't want the sight of me to bring it all back to him."

"Perhaps you're right."

"You sound doubtful."

Doctor Forsythe told Cluff, "I hear he's completed his arrangements about the estate."

"Has it made him happier?"

The doctor shook his head. He said, "Nothing will."

CHAPTER IV

Annie Croft said over the wire, "He's not here. He wasn't here when I came this morning." She demanded, "How do I know?" She paused and added, "But the dog's here. He hasn't taken the dog."

Constable Barker, in Cluff's room at Gunnarshaw police-station, put the phone down. He tiptoed to the door and looked out into the public office. He sidled past the policeman on the desk, cautiously, wanting to get out of the station without being seen by Inspector Mole. The man on the desk smiled, secure because it wasn't his business to answer the Inspector's questions about Cluff's activities.

Barker, permanently transferred to the C.I.D. after the Greensleeve affair,* wandered the streets of Gunnarshaw. He tried to put a date to it and he couldn't pinpoint the start of Cluff's remoteness, the Sergeant's malaise not so recent as this month but not so long-standing, perhaps, as the beginning of last month, the change Barker had felt in him falling somewhere between the two. He stood in the places where the Sergeant often stood, waiting for the Sergeant to appear. He stared at the familiar sights of the town and they weren't the same.

The day passed and it seemed to Barker that the Sergeant

---

*   *The Methods of Sergeant Cluff*

posted in the High Street was enough, Barker mimicking the Sergeant too much, but the Sergeant wasn't there and the Sergeant didn't come. The people stared at Barker and he knew they were comparing him with Cluff, wondering where Cluff was.

He went back to the police-station, unbuttoning his coat as he entered from the street. He shivered and said to the man on station duty, "It's cold enough for snow."

"At the end of October?" the man on the desk replied, but he hadn't been out in Gunnarshaw and, for all the good he'd done, Barker might as well not have been out either.

Barker crossed to the door of Cluff's room. He switched on the light, dispelling the gloom of early evening. The room was colder than out-of-doors, where the air at least was crisp, biting at the throat like wine. The room had a mustiness about it, permanently because its window was jammed beyond anyone's strength to open it, but in these last weeks the mustiness had grown stronger, the room more disused than normally. The constable looked at the calendar on the wall and the calendar confirmed what the policeman on the desk had said, the days slipping past unnoticed under the spell of the Sergeant's anticipation, Barker infected by Cluff.

The constable pushed the plug of the electric fire into its socket in the skirting-board and the fire made scratching noises, and clicks and scrapes, flashing blue sparks from the end of its element. It reddened and faded and recovered, small and rusty and round. Barker restrained himself with an effort from kicking it across the floor. He glanced at his watch, the days dark by tea-time now that the clocks had gone back. The fire spluttered finally and admitted defeat. Barker glared at the telephone and couldn't bring himself to ring up the cottage again, aware that Annie Croft would have left, certain that he'd get no reply.

He lost himself in conjecture and he missed the faint sound of the bell through the dividing wall. Someone coughed behind him and he jumped, his nerves on edge. Inspector Mole fixed him with a jaundiced eye, Mole's whole attitude a question-mark. Barker shook his head. The Inspector said, "I didn't think so," and shrugged his shoulders. "If I wasn't you I wish I was Cluff," the Inspector added. He went on, "I know now what they mean in Gunnarshaw when they talk about a 'Bobby's job.'"

Barker asked ineffectively, "Did you want him?"

"That was Lambert on the phone," the Inspector said and explained in the manner of a teacher to a backward child, "The village constable at Egilsby."

Barker gaped and the Inspector didn't believe that Barker had ever heard of Egilsby. He didn't realize for a moment that Barker wasn't gaping at him. He jumped more than Barker had done when the Inspector came into the room.

"Why?" Cluff said.

The Inspector whirled, angry with himself. He tried to pass off his loss of self-control. He said, "I thought we'd seen the end of you."

"Why?"

"I didn't recognize you without the dog." Mole stepped back before Cluff's advance from the door. "They've found the Colonel." Cluff halted. "But you wouldn't know he was missing."

"Where?"

"In the river."

The Sergeant sagged and Barker let out a long breath, wondering if this was what the Sergeant had been waiting for.

"You won't be needed," Mole said. "I thought I ought to tell you. You knew him."

"I knew him," Cluff said heavily, and went round the end of his table to sit in the chair behind it.

Barker stood by the window, the night outside growing grey with fog. He heard Inspector Mole telling the man on the desk, "Put my telephone through," and shortly afterwards the purr of the Inspector's little car driving out of the station yard. Barker glanced once or twice over his shoulder and the Sergeant was looking into space, an old man.

The Sergeant said, "Todd wasn't there."

"Who?"

"That's where I've been," Cluff said. "On the train. To where Todd lives. He was fifty miles from Egilsby yesterday. He's been fifty miles from Egilsby all day today."

"Todd?"

"The Colonel's nephew. The Colonel's heir."

"You don't think—?"

The Sergeant repeated, "But he wasn't there."

"I'll answer it," Barker interrupted, and Cluff wasn't making any effort to lift the telephone. Barker said, "Yes?" and then, "Hold on." He stayed close to the Sergeant, trying to catch the sense of the words coming over the line.

Doctor Forsythe asked, "You've heard?"

"Just now," Cluff replied.

"I've been going to get in touch with you all day," the doctor said.

"I'm listening."

"What the devil did you visit me for that night – four weeks ago was it, or five?"

"Is that what you're worried about?"

"Damn it, Caleb – what do you expect?" The doctor remained quiet for a while. "I don't want to be made a fool of."

"Would I do that?"

"Look," the doctor said. "I'm ashamed of myself for ringing. I couldn't stop myself."

"You're not making it easier," the Sergeant told him.

The doctor's voice rose: "I was there when they pulled him out."

"How was that?"

"They rang me up."

"Miss Ambler?"

"That maid, Betty Metcalfe—"

"I see."

"It was legitimate. The daughter needed something to calm her."

"She's never struck me as the hysterical type."

"She blamed herself—"

"Poor woman!"

"—for allowing him to go out alone."

"Had he never to be free from her?"

"I stayed on. Lambert had a search-party combing the fields – I'm telling you what you know already?"

"Lambert reports to Mole. Nobody's told me this concerns the C.I.D."

"I wanted to be on the spot. If he'd had a seizure of some sort—"

"Of course."

The doctor said desperately, "He drowned. But it's more than possible – a sudden heart attack – after he slipped into the water if not before."

"Do you feel better now you've talked to me?"

"I didn't want you to think otherwise, Caleb."

"I'll take your word for it."

"In any case, after all those hours in the water—"

"The river must be in spate."

"He'd gone downstream during the night, nearly a couple of miles."

"I know what that means."

"He wasn't a pretty sight."

The doctor added, "I can only speak as I found it. I wouldn't have rung if it had been anybody but you."

"I won't mention it."

"Thanks."

"Have they sent for Todd?"

"Yes." The doctor sounded contrite. "You were right. The dale won't be the same without an Ambler."

The police-station was very silent, as silent as the street outside. It occurred to Barker that nine nights out of ten they could have closed the doors of the police-station and locked up without anyone being the wiser. He could almost hear the duty constable's pen scratching and after a while that stopped too. Occasionally feet shuffled in the outer office as the duty constable eased himself in his chair. Cluff didn't move and neither did Barker.

Barker couldn't stand it any longer. He said, making a statement of it, "You haven't got your car." He asked, "Shall I get hold of the motor-unit?"

"I'd rather walk," Cluff told him.

CHAPTER V

A key jarred in the lock of the back door downstairs, Annie Croft arriving from the hamlet where she lived, three-quarters of a mile away. He heard Annie talking to Clive in the kitchen, Clive whimpering in reply. The door remained open a little longer, until Clive went outside, and then closed.

The Sergeant lay in bed, angry with himself, dissatisfied, almost a week gone by since Colonel Ambler's death, Todd in possession at the Hall. He traced Annie Croft's movements by the sounds she made, water running from a tap, the kettle banged on the Calor-gas stove. The handle of the ash-bucket clanked metallically against its rim. A shovel grated. A brush bumped against the sides of the fireplace in the room below. He listened to Annie making the fire and her movements as she laid the table for breakfast.

He pushed Jenet off the bed and as soon as he was out of bed the cat jumped back, digging under the crumpled covers to the warm under-sheet. He gazed through the diamond-shaped, leaded panes of the dormer window, at the rain and the pastures beyond the wall of his garden. The pastures were black with water and the moors into which the pastures merged dark-toned, lacking brilliance.

He forced himself to shave and wash and dress. In the living-room a newspaper lay by his plate. He opened the

paper, not a national daily, a copy of the local weekly, printed
in Gunnarshaw, its pages irregularly shuffled together, creased.
He folded it back in the middle and from the headlines and
the long columns of print he thought the Editor must rarely
have had the satisfaction of news such as this. The Sergeant
had no heart to read but he read all the same. The account
of the Colonel's funeral, of outstanding interest in any case
to the paper's circulation, gained immeasurably from the
drama of the events preceding the funeral. The record didn't
end with the list of mourners and organizations represented,
with the careful specification of the details on each card
accompanying each wreath and spray of flowers. A history of
the deceased's family, far from concise, of its achievements and
honours, its importance and its influence in the countryside,
flowed naturally from a biography of the Colonel's life. The
Colonel's son was named, with expressions of regret mingled
with sentiments of patriotism, but Cluff's name wasn't there.

Annie Croft pushed past him and slapped a full plate on
the table. He handed the newspaper to her. He said, "Why did
you bring it?"

"I haven't seen one lying about."

He sat down and began his breakfast.

Annie Croft said defiantly, "You ought to have gone."

"I don't like funerals."

"What's the matter with you these days?"

They didn't speak to each other again. He finished his
breakfast and moved to the chair by the fire, its flames reflected
in the polished oak furniture and the glinting brasses. Jenet,
chased from the bed by Annie, contemplated him stonily from
the chair across the hearth, the cat's eyes as hard as agate.

Clive, returned from his excursion outdoors, stretched on the rug between them.

Smoke curled lazily from the Sergeant's pipe. His eyes were heavy and a little red. His eyelids drooped over his eyes and he jerked them open. His head nodded on to his chest. He lolled slackly in the chair, very still, the pipe clenched between his teeth.

A gleam of watery sunlight, splitting the cloudwrack, strayed through the window into the cottage, barring the room with yellow, motes of dust floating airily in its rays. Annie Croft said, "Nobody told me." The Sergeant groped down the side of the chair for his pipe. Annie Croft explained, "That you'd retired."

He struck a match and fit the cold dottle in the pipe-bowl: "What time is it?"

"Coming up for half-eleven."

"Barker'll let me know if I'm wanted."

She sniffed: "You'll have your dinner before I go?"

"I'm not hungry."

When she was safely in the kitchen he went upstairs, the cottage small, one of its two bedrooms converted into a bathroom, a walled-up space hardly more than a cupboard at the end of the landing. He rooted amongst the junk in the box-room until he found a canvas tube containing the segments of a fishing-rod. He untied the tapes holding the tube closed and shook out the rod, screwing it together, testing the reel, sliding the line between finger and thumb, winding it in again. He discovered a tin box, containing artificial flies, and a wickerwork creel. He remembered a net but he couldn't find it and he gave up looking for it.

Whether he wanted it or not his dinner was ready for him. He ate it obediently, missing the softening of Annie Croft's features when he had his back to her. Afterwards he got the rod and the creel. He fought a battle between inclination and what he tried to believe was duty. One or the other won, but he didn't know which. He went into the bathroom impulsively and stuffed his razor and shaving-brush, a stick of shaving-soap and a toothbrush into his pocket. At the bottom of the stairs he saw Annie, out of the corner of his eye, filling the doorway of the kitchen, not from top to bottom but from side to side, dumpy, big-breasted, her cheeks glowing.

He cleared his throat. He muttered, "Leave plenty out for the cat." He jerked his head sideways at Clive. The dog's tail rose and the dog came to him quickly. The sound Annie made might have expressed anything, contempt, disbelief, a conviction that the Sergeant had gone wrong in his head. She gazed pointedly at the creel slung from his shoulder, the rod tucked under his arm, the bulge in his pocket:

"What have I to tell them if they ring up from Gunnarshaw?"

"I've gone fishing."

The rod and the creel bounced on the floor of the car, nudging the Sergeant's walking-stick. Clive leaned heavily against him as he guided the car out of the shed and into the lane. The car protested, an antipathy between itself and its driver. It wandered constantly towards the roadside ditch, determined on self-destruction rather than submit to the Sergeant's heavy-handed torment. Cluff pulled its nose this way and that, vaguely aware of the road, making a regal progress in the middle of the road. The car toiled up the rises and Cluff could have walked faster. A blue cloud of exhaust smoke trailed in its rear, offending his nostrils, polluting the rain-washed air on the moor-tops as he forced the car over the watershed between one dale and the next. The grace of God not his own skill kept the Sergeant safe on the long descent. He strained back in his seat, his body stiff, his foot braced on the brake-pedal, clutching the bucking steering-wheel, silently cursing all things mechanical.

The ground to the left sloped steeply, forming a narrow valley like an axe-cut in the land, its bottom wooded, the trees bare and black. The silver of a river glistened through the branches, crossed, before the river vanished for a stretch, by the thread of a footbridge. Downstream, where the river reappeared, a church tower loomed over the miniature buildings of a village, dwarfed by distance. The more he dropped from the fells the wider the river, the trees sparser than at first sight, the valley sides broken and rocky, the opposite bank of the river climbing more abruptly than this one.

The Sergeant managed to stop the car, not behind the still figure leaning on the wall but a hundred yards or so past it. He got out of the car and looked back at the long body arched against the wall, its elbows on the top-stones, its chin in the palms of its hands, its eyes fixed on the river. Cluff's boots rang on the metalled road.

"Canon Staveley," Cluff said.

"Canon Staveley!" Cluff repeated.

The Rector's head came up. A spasm travelled through his body and one of the stones on the wall fell into the field on the other side, rolling a little way in the wet grass. A pale, blood-drained face, lined and thin, the eyes pouched, the lips working inaudibly, stared into Cluff's face. The Rector's mackintosh outdid Cluff's Burberry in age and stains, the clothes under the mackintosh older than Cluff's, the jacket belonging to one suit, the trousers to another. Unsuspended socks wrinkled above unpolished shoes, dirty skin visible through a hole in one heel.

Side by side they looked over the wall, the country rain-swept and grim, at a path running up from the village along the river-bank, the river and the road converging but still separated by the fields, the river ominous, forbidding, apart from the river nothing alive or moving within the range of their vision. The Rector trembled and went on trembling. The river roared. The afternoon was cold, but not so cold as that.

"I'm going to the village," Cluff said. "Can I give you a lift?"

The Sergeant returned to his car. The Rector's coat-tails flew and the Rector clapped a hand on his hat, almost dislodged by his mute rejection of the Sergeant's offer. The Rector ran for a break in the wall, through the break on to a footpath, out of sight into a small wood.

The car coasted through the village, past the drive to the Hall, the lych-gate into the churchyard, the entrance to the Rectory, between the cottages and farms. It rounded the bend by Sam Rycroft's store and sub-post office and stopped at the foot of a humpbacked stone bridge carrying the road across the river. The car had an inn on one side of it, a village green, with the white finger of a maypole erect at its far boundary, on the other. A round-bellied, short man, with a bald head and a fat face, in his shirt-sleeves, appeared at the door of the inn.

The Sergeant reversed on to the forecourt of the inn. Clive jumped out and made for the river-bank, through a space between the gable of the inn and the foundations of the bridge. Cluff unloaded his gear and his stick.

The fat man said, "Wonders never cease."

"It's fishing weather," Cluff told him.

Ted Hardacre said, "It's been fishing weather for years. We haven't seen you up here to catch owt."

"What's to stop me? I did plenty when I was younger."

"It's not what's stopped thee," Ted Hardacre pointed out, deliberately lapsing into his broadest accent to give emphasis and meaning to his words. "It's what's started thee again."

Cluff shouldered his rod with one hand and swung his stick in the other. His creel banged against his hip: "I'll be back."

"I'm sure on it."

CHAPTER VI

In Rycroft's shop they heard Cluff's car coming while it was still a mile away. Sam Rycroft's knife poised. He waited until the car, blasting the peace of the village with a noise loud enough to wake the dead, passed the window. He said, "By—!" and words failed him.

Betty Metcalfe remarked, "I know what I'd do with it if it was mine."

Sam stuck the point of the knife in a slab of lard. He came from behind the counter, rubbing his hands on his apron, muttering, "There can't be two alike." He stepped through the shop door and peered towards the stone bridge. He asked, of the village at large, "What's Caleb Cluff doing up here?"

"You've got eyes in your head," Betty Metcalfe said, at his shoulder.

"Fishing? I'm not that simple."

Ted Hardacre went back into the "George and Dragon." Cluff rounded the gable of the inn, out of view on to the river-bank. Betty said to Sam Rycroft, "I shouldn't like to think you were missing anything." She added, her voice louder, "I haven't got all day—"

She set off back up the road for the Hall, her basket filled. Josh Lambert propped himself on the inside of a garden gate, the cottage behind him no different from the other cottages except that the silver badge of the County Constabulary shone on the wall over its door. "Didn't he call in?" Betty said. Josh raised eyes as placid as a cow's. Betty told the constable, "He's gone up the river," and Lambert nodded, his calm undisturbed.

Apart from Josh she had the road to herself but she thought her solitude was more apparent than real. She imagined eyes watching her from the windows of the cottages and the farm-houses, their owners hiding behind the curtains. She felt herself different, and the village different. The people of Egilsby didn't talk much at the best of times but had they drawn further into their shells since the Colonel's death? She laughed at herself and her laughter wasn't sincere. She wished she didn't work at the Hall and why shouldn't she work at the Hall?

The Rectory stood as decrepit as its occupant; the grass in the churchyard, dying back, matted the graves. She'd never been an introspective girl, accustomed all her life to the grimness and the greyness of the village, fortified against weakness by her environment. She couldn't get the picture of the Rector out of her mind, in church this last Sunday, stumbling through the service, losing himself in the middle of his sermon, daily thinner and more drawn. She couldn't see the Rector, either around the Rectory or the church. She didn't believe he found much happiness in his birdwatching and his books, not now, but Anthea Ambler wasn't the only woman in the world and surely someone would have had him if he'd looked about a bit.

Her feet dragged up the drive to the Hall. The Hall lowered at her, its windows mullioned, its chimney-stacks ornate, ivy shrouding the black stone. Its gardens were autumn-drab, its shrubberies dull green, most of the trees that sheltered it coniferous, equally without colour.

She walked round the Hall, in at the back. She put the basket on the kitchen table and started to take off her coat. The sound of voices, a man's and a woman's, warned her that the door into the passage leading to the front of the house was open. She crossed to the door to shut it and a shadow moved by the panelling enclosing the staircase. She grabbed Sims by the shoulder and pulled him roughly into the kitchen.

He grinned at her, a knowledge, a salaciousness, in his eyes. He looked her up and down, as if her clothing was no barrier to his vision. She said, "Your job's in the garden."

He laughed. He replied, "She won't let Todd alone." He rolled his eyes round the kitchen and he included in the kitchen the Hall and the Ambler estate. He told Betty, "Todd hasn't got all this for nothing." He asked, "What goes on at nights? You sleep in. You must have heard something."

"Her father hasn't been dead much more than a week."

"She's a lot of time to make up."

"What of it?"

"I've seen them through the windows—"

"He'll marry her, won't he?"

"He's got all he wants without that."

"Can't you think of anything else?"

"They're cousins."

"It doesn't make any difference."

"Not to her. He'd have to be far gone to take her for a wife."

"He owes her something. She got him in here—"

"She couldn't get him out now if she tried."

Betty put a kettle on the fire: "There's always the Rector to fall back on."

"Not after Todd." Sims's slack lips were moist. "You've all the fun—"

"Stop bothering me!"

He flung at her, on his way to the garden, "What's up? Did you want him for yourself?" He suggested, "Try the Rector. The Rector's at the last gasp."

"No more than you are."

"You'd be surprised."

"I would if I heard of a girl going out with you." She arranged the tray and emptied the kettle into the silver teapot. She rattled the tray in the passage and trod heavily, making as much noise as she could. She balanced the tray with one hand on a lifted knee and knocked at the sitting-room door. She heard quiet shuffling noises.

Inside the room Todd reclined in an armchair, his legs extended, his ankles crossed, wriggling his toes so that the caps of his shoes danced a slow measure. The chair was wide enough for him to have one of his hands in a trouser pocket and the hand jingled coins. He had his head thrown back, his eyes on the plaster ceiling, his lips pursed like those of a man whistling silently to himself. Anthea Ambler, on the rug by her chair, stared at her feet, her hollow cheeks very pink in contrast to her usual pallor, her thin lips slightly parted, breathing quickly.

"Put it down," Todd said. His eyes slipped away from the ceiling and roved over Betty, the look in his eyes like the look in Walt Sims's eyes. He let his eyes stay on the maid, not troubling about his cousin. Something amused him and he wasn't trying to hide his amusement. He made his amusement plain.

Betty Metcalfe carried the tray to a table by Todd's chair. Todd said lazily, his tone bored, "You haven't been long. What's the news in the village?" He added, "If there is any news," and he looked past her at Anthea Ambler, his amusement more obvious.

"The Sergeant's come," Betty replied, and she heard Anthea Ambler move jerkily.

"Who?" Todd said, without interest.

"Sergeant Cluff. From Gunnarshaw."

"A friend of yours?"

Anthea Ambler had her hand to her mouth, her body tense, her eyes fixed on Todd's face. Todd was saying, as Betty left the room, "Will you pour, or shall I?" and Anthea Ambler hadn't moved again when Betty closed the door. The maid listened, her ear to the panelling. For a while she couldn't hear anything and when she did she could only distinguish between Todd's voice and the woman's, not what they were saying.

CHAPTER VII

"Why don't you go for a walk?" Todd said.

"You'll come?"

"Me?" and he put into the word all his contempt for the country.

Todd balanced his saucer on his knee, relaxed, basking in the warmth and the dimness. "At least," he said, "sit down."

Anthea Ambler couldn't sit down. She couldn't stay still, overcome by reaction to her stillness while Betty had been in the room. She wandered, without a purpose, fingering the objects with which the room was decorated, the ashtrays and pieces of porcelain, straightening them, setting them exactly to rights. Todd said, "For God's sake!" without much force, irritated but too lethargic to allow his irritation to get the better of him.

She didn't look round at him. She continued to drift, aimlessly. She said, "When?" and her voice was pleading, pregnant with petition.

"Don't they expect a proper period of mourning?"

"I don't care!"

"I'm here with you. In the same house."

"You promised."

"Have I denied it?"

"If it hadn't been for me—"

"I know," and he sounded a little weary. He said again, "Go for a walk. It'll do you good."

She moaned and he knew she'd go, because she was too restless to remain. He closed his eyes, hoping to add decision to her irresolution. He heard her for a few minutes more and he kept his eyes closed, aware that she was staring at him, refusing to capitulate any further to her importunity. She crept, little by little, closer to the door. He heard the door open and he breathed a sigh of relief.

A flurry in the passage to the kitchen startled Anthea Ambler and there was nothing, no one, in the passage. She seized a hat and a coat from the stand by the front door. She walked rapidly down the drive and stopped where the drive joined the road, wanting to go to the village, unable to face the village.

The wind blew the rain into her face, not in a steady downpour but in gusts. The clouds raced across the darkening sky. Her step quickened and she began to pant, compelling herself up the hill, the village behind her, trying to empty her mind, her head woolly with thoughts. She'd seen herself as she was for too long not to see herself now as she was. She clung to his promises and her faith in his promises waned. She had to hold to his promises because she'd nothing else to hold to.

She didn't see where she was going. She didn't realize how far she'd gone from the village. She couldn't avoid the man who stepped into the road from the mouth of the path going down to the river, too late when she saw him to escape. She compared him swiftly with Todd and the nakedness, the futility, of his aspirations gave her courage. She began to turn away as he was saying, "Don't go," the hope of flight reviving in her, supported by her certainty that he wouldn't dare attempt to stop her.

She halted abruptly and he couldn't have said it, but he had said it. And if he'd said it, why shouldn't he have said it? All he'd said was "The Colonel—" and if there was meaning in his voice she'd imagined the meaning.

"Look," she heard.

In spite of herself she couldn't ignore him. He had an arm raised, pointing over the wall, across the pastures. A man squatted on the bank of the river, with his back to the road, too far away for his features to be recognized even if he'd had his face towards them. He had a dog with him and the back and the dog told her all she needed to know. But she didn't need telling and the impression she had of a rod poking over the water didn't help her. She dismissed the rod even as she thought of it.

She gazed at the river and at the man by the river and not for a long time did she remember the man beside her. She couldn't tear her eyes from the river and the Canon was looking where she looked, a communication between herself and the Canon. Her heart began to thump before Canon Staveley spoke and she might have heard the words as he said them or she might have heard them afterwards or she might not have heard them at all, the words passing between him and her by some kind of telepathy. Canon Staveley said, "The evening your father disappeared—"

She stood rigid, seeing him without seeing him, feeling the battle inside him between love and horror, his face disembodied, floating in front of her eyes, a transparent screen through which she could still see the man by the river. The weariness of the face weighed on her and she suffocated, the face sleepless, its flesh dissolving, little more than a death's-head, only the eyes alight.

"What has happened between us?" he said and the rest of him joined his face, forcing her to admit the deterioration the village must have noticed but in which she hadn't been interested.

She thought, "When was there ever anything between us?" and who'd understood, even before her father died, that she and the Rector would become husband and wife? Who except the Rector, and the village, and perhaps her father who understood, too, that she could wait to have a life of her own until it suited her father's convenience?

"What do you see in him?" the Rector was asking.

She couldn't have hidden it, not in a village like Egilsby, and Betty would have talked, or Sims would have talked, and hadn't she wanted them to talk, to broadcast to the village and to the world what there was between herself and Todd? She was safer for what the village knew, for what the Rector knew, the bonds between herself and Todd the stronger. She said, "There isn't anything you can do."

The engine of a motor vehicle droned in the distance, in one of the many hollows into which the road dipped. If she heard it the Rector didn't hear it. The Rector's lips framed the single word, "Cluff."

He had her sleeve in his grip before she could stop him. "Is there no hope?" he asked. "No hope at all?" And was he holding her or she him as she shook her head wildly? He sagged and she read agony in his eyes and she said "Cluff?"

too, suddenly afraid of what he meant by "Cluff," of why he was there on the road spying on Cluff.

The engine belonged to a Land-Rover. The driver of the Land-Rover saw them in the road and stamped a foot on his brake. He recognized them both, in a kind of embrace, dragging each other out of his way, the Rector's hands on Anthea Ambler, her hands on the Rector. The farmer's foot slipped off the pedal and he'd gone past them. He looked back over his shoulder before he rounded the bend because he still couldn't credit the evidence of his eyes.

She was racing along the road, pursuing the Land-Rover and she couldn't catch it. The Rector ran after her, shouting, and her brain was chaos, but order came out of chaos. She shouldn't have been surprised to meet the Rector on the road. The Rector was always on the road, or in the fields, his binoculars round his neck, moving like a ghost, hidden, slipping from cover to cover, studying his birds. He hadn't his binoculars today but when hadn't he had his binoculars, when before her father died?

The Rector panted behind her, "I can't go on."

She ran and she asked herself as she ran, "Did he love me as much as that?" She must have asked the question aloud because she was sure he was saying, "What greater proof could I have given you?"

He had some hidden reserve of power she didn't possess. She couldn't outrun him and she faltered, breathless, her strength ebbing. He added to his previous statement, elaborating it, "Without you I can't go on."

"But with me?"

His hands covered his face. His voice was like a groan

through his fingers. He said, "I don't know. I don't know!"

She began to walk. She said, "Give me time. Please give me time."

Her steps receded. He didn't go with her and he couldn't bear to watch her go. He returned to the wall. Cluff sat in the same place, in exactly the same position. The Rector, no less than the rest of Egilsby, came to grips with the reasons for Cluff's presence. Couldn't a man, if he was a policeman, spend a quiet afternoon fishing in the river? Canon Staveley didn't believe it. No one in Egilsby believed it, except perhaps Todd at the Hall to whom fishing and all the occupations of the countryside were equally a mystery.

Self-interest battled with conscience in the Rector's mind, Cluff the cause of the crisis. So much done already and was it all to be thrown away, nothing to come of it, after the hard years, the barren years, the years of sacrifice? Did the Rector think of what he had missed or of what Anthea Ambler had missed, or of what could have been for both of them together had she been free from the Colonel?

The stones of the wall supporting the Rector projected in places, not deliberately a stile but serving the purpose of a stile. The Hall didn't matter to him, nor the Ambler estate, and it wouldn't be difficult. The wall made it easy for him. He could put his feet on the stones and climb over the wall. He could cross the field on the other side of the wall and the field beyond that field. He knew Cluff wouldn't move while he was making his way towards Cluff. How could he do it, destroying what had been the whole object of his life? What had the letter of the law to do with penitence, the sentence of a court with the sufferings of humanity?

Anthea Ambler filled the Rector's world and Anthea Ambler fled to Todd, away from Canon Staveley. She burst into the sitting-room at the Hall, Todd half-asleep, the room dim, the tea-tray gone. She said, "Robert!" as she ran to him, her coat falling to the floor, her hat dropping beside it.

He sprang to his feet after her first sentences. He turned the key in the lock on the door. He drew the curtains across the windows to shut out what was left of the day. He returned to his chair and held out his arms.

She went to him, hesitantly at first but flinging herself on him in the end. She buried her head in his shoulder. His arms closed round her and they stayed round her.

He said, "Now," and strained his ears to make sense of her muffled words, her mouth gagged against him. His lips tightened and her brittle hair rasped the underside of his chin.

CHAPTER VIII

The path from the village began by the bridge, round the gable of the "George and Dragon" from the road. It ran under the trees growing by the river, the houses of Egilsby not far away over the grass. The river flowed straight in the bottom of the valley and the road to Gunnarshaw branched to the top of the fells, the farms and cottages for as far as they stretched bordering the road. The farther a man went along the path the broader the extent of the fields between himself and the road. The river-bank opened up into pastures but only on this side, on the other a continuous, almost vertical scar on whose precipitous slopes stunted bushes clung precariously.

Farther upstream the land on the Egilsby bank rose suddenly into a hill, the hill sliced through by the river, the face of the cut forming, with the opposite scar, a narrow gorge through which the river flowed. The nature of the path changed. From a track trodden in the fields by the river it became a ribbon of concrete poured amongst the rocks in the gorge, aiming at a smooth, level passage round the base of the hill, the hill sheer on its left, the water rushing on its right. In times of flood the water overflowed the path, restricted by the gorge, leaving the path slippery with moss and weed. The concrete had crumbled and cracked and in some parts fallen altogether from its bed, leaving gaps in the path. The path needed care even in summer until it reached the pastures higher up the dale. In winter the path was dangerous to the unwary and the river waited for those who lost their footing.

Cluff sat on a stone at the point where the path left the field and started into the gorge. The wind blew down the funnel of the gorge and whenever his hat and Burberry began to dry a new shower fell to make them wet again. His rod rested in a forked stick he'd stuck into the ground and his line curved into a half-circle in the wind. A float bobbed in the ripples of a deeper pool where the line vanished into the water. His creel hadn't been opened. He wasn't fly-fishing. If he had bait on his hook it hadn't helped him to a catch. Clive sat on that side of the Sergeant protected by him from the wind. They had their eyes on the float as if hypnotized by it.

The shadows lengthened. The wind grew colder, the flurries of rain more icy, the river louder in the gathering night.

Clive's fur bristled. The dog's head turned slightly. The dog tensed. The Sergeant murmured to the dog, without shifting a muscle. A voice said, "Nay – you can do better than that."

Cluff said, "If I set my mind to it."

A third pair of eyes additional to Cluff's eyes and the dog's eyes fixed on the red-banded, white float rising and falling in the river. Josh Lambert's thumbs, under his cape, hooked into the waistband of his trousers. He was as big as Cluff, built like Cluff, as solid. His helmet added to his height.

"It'll be pitch-black soon," the constable said.

"I'm not likely to fall in."

"If they haven't been biting they won't be biting now."

Cluff asked, "Where did you find him?"

"Past the stone bridge, where the river bends at the far side of the green."

Cluff's eyes came up from the float and stared over the river. Cluff said, "There's someone up there."

"That'll be Christy."

"Poaching?"

"He takes some getting near to."

"It's a good day for it."

"It does you for fishing."

Josh Lambert stubbed the toe of his boot in soft soil. He went on, "The doctor was with us."

"I know."

"You would."

"I know where Todd was too."

"That's more than I know, except that he wasn't at the Hall."

"He's got it now."

"Changing his name by poll isn't going to make Todd an Ambler. The Colonel ought to have seen that."

"It's in the will?"

"So they say."

"Lucky for Todd the Colonel got things fixed up in time."

"Only just."

"Eh?"

"A few months ago. They had Betty Metcalfe in for a witness."

"Well?"

Lambert said, "The Colonel was sick. He had to be sick. Nothing else would have made him have anything to do with the Todds."

"His sister died years ago."

"He never spoke to her again after she married Todd's father."

"It changed things when Dick Ambler was killed."

"The Amblers can't go on for ever."

"They've managed it for centuries."

"They've had a good run then."

The Sergeant groped for his rod. He began to reel in the line. "The path's not all that close to the edge of the bank."

Josh Lambert looked past Cluff, at the concrete footway rounding the base of the hill in the gorge. "It is there."

"The Colonel knew it well enough."

"He wouldn't stay in," Lambert said. "He didn't let the weather stop him. She did her best but she couldn't control him in that. I can't say different."

"She's lost by it," Cluff said, and they didn't need to put a name to the pronoun, Anthea Ambler clear in both their minds.

"Not if she marries Todd," Lambert said.

"Maybe not."

Lambert said, "If you ask me she's gained. She might have caught the Rector but she'd precious little hope of anyone else at her age."

"She's no beauty."

"That's not the end of it. She's had things her own way too long. I wouldn't want her."

"Todd'll find out."

"There'll be trouble if he does."

"She stuck to her father."

"She saw herself doing it."

Cluff unscrewed the rod.

Lambert said, "The Colonel fell in," emphasizing the verb.

Cluff put the segments of the rod in their case. "He must have done. You pulled him out."

"He was eighteen hours or so in the water."

The Sergeant shouldered his creel and picked up his walking-stick. "You're going back to the village?"

"Aye."

They walked together down the river-bank.

Josh Lambert said, "I looked – up there on the path. If there'd ever been anything to see it'd have gone by the time I got there."

"Was it dark when they told you?"

"They didn't know he hadn't come in. She'd been lying down upstairs. When she found out she went to look for him herself."

"That's reasonable."

"It's no skin off my nose, Caleb," Josh Lambert said. "If you can make anything of it, I can't."

The river foamed over the rocks in its bed. The rocks protruded from the surface of the water, jagged and sharp, the current hurling itself against them.

Cluff said, "After a man's been in that you couldn't tell what had happened to him."

"Not unless he'd been shot or had his head cut off."

"It only happens like that in books."

"What does?"

"Work it out for yourself."

CHAPTER IX

M en sat on the benches round the wall of the bar in the "George and Dragon". They'd glass mugs in their hands, pipes in their mouths. Hardacre pulled the handle of the beer-pump, busy with replenishments. They talked slowly, with long pauses between the sentences, each man considering before he spoke.

Someone said, "Isn't he off back to Gunnarshaw?"

"With an empty creel?"

"He used to come over from Cluff's Head as a lad. He could catch fish when I couldn't."

"He's worsened then."

"I've seen him and Dick Ambler pulling them out one after the other. They knew what they were about, those two."

"He'd no side on him, hadn't Dick."

"There wasn't a better shot in the dale. When him and Caleb Cluff got together on the moor—"

"Look what we've got at the Hall instead of Dick."

"The good ones like Dick going—"

"It isn't Caleb's fault Dick's where he is."

"It won't be Caleb's fault if Todd stays where he is."

"A blessing the Colonel's gone."

"It beats me how he lasted as long as he did."

"With Todd to come after him? Nay, he'd hang on while

he could."

A man asked Hardacre, "What's got into Caleb anyway? If he's stopping he ought to be in here. Do we stink or something?"

"Caleb?" Sam Rycroft said, coming into the bar from the passage. "I've just passed him. He's off over the bridge with that dog of his."

"He's not!"

"It's right."

"He wouldn't be out for pleasure on a night like this."

"He's after something."

"What do you make of it?"

"I make nothing of what Caleb Cluff does. It's safer not to try."

The Sergeant leaned on the parapet of the bridge, in the V-shaped space off the carriageway on top of one of the piers, the blackness below him flecked with white. The village loomed to his left, blacker than the night, the masses of its cottages more black for the occasional contrast of a lighted window. Minute spots of yellow high up on the moors marked the positions of isolated farms. The moors hugged the village closer than in the daytime, pressing in on the village, cutting it off from the rest of the world, keeping it private and inviolate, self-contained. He felt a part of the village not of the world beyond the village. Over there, where the moors shaded into the dark sky, was Cluff's Head where he'd been born. He couldn't understand, sometimes, how he'd come to leave Cluff's Head, how he'd found his way not merely into the police force but into the plain-clothes branch. He was nearer to the people in the village than he was to the people outside the village. If he didn't get to the bottom of this no one would.

Clive's nose nuzzled his leg. He asked himself, get to the bottom of what? What had he begun? What had he to go on? Would he have been here at all if Dick Ambler hadn't been his friend? He hadn't the impartiality, the impersonality, his profession demanded. He could feel for Anthea Ambler, concerned for her father, abetting the Colonel, in spite of himself, in the preservation of Amblers in the dale, in the perpetuity of the Ambler estate in Ambler hands. He felt with the Colonel, reduced to extending the hospitality of the Hall to Todd, no other son after Dick, no other nephew. He began even to feel for Todd, though he knew Todd now, wondering whether he was condemning Todd out of hand, finding nothing good in Todd because Todd had been born in a city, raised in a city, and everything about him proclaimed his attachment to all the Sergeant hated and despised, the new life instead of the old, the false values instead of the true.

The Sergeant stared into the dark and he saw too much, he condemned too easily, forgetting the Colonel's quarrel with his sister, who was Todd's mother, the care Anthea Ambler would have had to exercise to bring Todd and the Colonel together, no fault of Todd's, Todd suffering from the disputes of the older generation. He could see the Colonel's doubts and if he'd been the Colonel the Colonel's uncertainties would have been his uncertainties, the Colonel's consolation that a will could be altered his consolation, but would the Colonel have been right about Todd, would he have been right?

The Sergeant stiffened in the night. He began to walk along the road and the Colonel's will couldn't be altered now. The

white walls were ghostly, the trunk of a tree growing by itself
a spectre. An owl screeched suddenly, shattering the silence,
leaving a deeper silence in its wake. Clive hugged his heels,
the dog subdued. The Sergeant cursed himself and where was
the molehill he couldn't, if he tried, make into a mountain?
But the country spoke to him and he went on.

A sliver of light rimmed the doorway of the ramshackle
cottage built on a step of the moor, huddling for protection
against the breast of the moor. The Sergeant stamped the mud
of the track from the road off his boots. He shouted above the
wind, at the full strength of his lungs, "Christy!"

The thickness of the walls through which he passed was
thicker than himself. The room he entered occupied the whole
space of the cottage on the ground floor. A flight of steps at
the back, unenclosed, no more than a rough ladder, led to a
trap-like hole in the sagging ceiling. Old sacks served as carpet
on the shaling flags. A single lamp burnt on a bare, wooden
table. Indeterminate heaps of rubbish piled in the corners.
Wire snares hung on pegs, jumbled with tattered nets and old,
ragged coats. Christy crouched by a rusty range, on an upended
box, as filthy as the house, as smelly and disintegrating, his
hands and the knife in his hands bloodstained. Christy flung
the naked body of the hare he'd been skinning on to the table
and the furred skin on to a heap of other skins. He said, "I saw
you by the river." Cluff sat down on the only chair.

"Where's Lambert now?" Christy asked.

"He won't bother you."

"I've nowt to do with Lambert."

"I thought as much."

Christy's face was the colour of old brick, leathery, cured

by the weather into hide. His eyes were very clear and blue, their lightness and sparkle startling. He looked at Clive and his eyes softened, filling with longing and regret. "Where's your dog?" Cluff asked.

"She died."

"She was old."

"Aye."

Cluff said, "There's a new litter at Cluff's Head. I'll get one for you."

"I don't need bribing."

"What me and Dick got to know you taught us."

"It's a long while since."

"Too long."

Christy said, and Cluff knew he was speaking of the Colonel, "He wasn't any older than I am. His heart was as strong as mine."

"Who's saying it wasn't?"

"Isn't she saying so?" and again the old man didn't have to explain who he meant.

"Is that why he fell in the river?"

"He never fell in."

"Did you see him?"

The old man shook his head.

Cluff said, "Once in he'd not be able to get out."

"Not with the river as it was that day."

"Conscious or unconscious."

"It wouldn't matter."

Cluff listened to the howl of the wind and the creak of the shutter over the one window. "I saw her," Christy said.

"She went to look for him."

"Not then."

"You didn't tell Lambert."

"I knew you'd come."

"The two of them together?"

"Didn't the Colonel have enough of her at the Hall?"

"I'd think so," Cluff said.

"They're good dogs," Christy said, his eyes on Clive. "There's none of better breeding."

"I won't forget," Cluff promised. He asked, "Where?"

"In the fields by the Hall."

"And you?"

"On the moorside over the road."

"It was a poor day. There wouldn't be anybody out."

"One man was."

Cluff nodded. Christy was behind him at the door. Cluff said, "You should have let me know about the dog."

"You'd stopped coming up here."

Cluff sighed.

"I've nowt else for company," Christy said.

Cluff replied, "I'm not so much better off."

He heard Christy shout, "Ask the Rector."

The Sergeant walked back to the village. The weather didn't keep the Colonel in, nor Christy, nor the Rector, the rest of Egilsby perhaps, except in emergency, but not those three. The Colonel with his thoughts, Christy poaching, the Rector with his birds, the Rector with his unfulfilled dreams. The river visible from the road, the road visible from the moor above the road, what was moving on the road and the moor hidden from the river, unless by chance, by the walls and the background of the fells. But the gorge the river flowed through private, to the road and to the moor, to the fields, to much of the river-bank above and below.

The windows of the "George and Dragon" glowed with invitation. He could hear voices as he passed outside the bar parlour. His dog looked up at him and they ignored the door of the inn. They went on, round the corner by the shop, quietly in case Josh Lambert lurked in the shadows.

CHAPTER X

Canon Staveley's housekeeper had a view through the window of the Rectory kitchen, across the vegetable garden and the field beyond, of the river-bank. She stood by the window, in the dusk, glowering at the weeds in the garden. Her eyes strayed constantly from the window to the clock on the kitchen mantelpiece. Oldish, small, thin, she had a sharp face, shrewish and bitter. She was impatient and her impatience made her angry.

She saw Josh Lambert on the river-bank and she knew, as everyone did, Josh's companion, identification doubly sure because of the dog with Caleb Cluff. She wasn't watching for Josh or the Sergeant but for her employer. Canon Staveley's comings and goings were unpredictable, his lack of consideration complete. The housekeeper's foot tapped on the linoleum. The Rector had been bad enough before but he'd been worse these last days, vaguer than ever, more forgetful, preoccupied.

The night closed in. She stayed in the dark, her foot still tapping, not switching on the light for a long time. In the end she had to put the light on in order to see the clock. The clock sent her to the front door and men outside on the road, bound for the "George and Dragon," confirmed the time the clock showed. The housekeeper's lips curled. She was strict in her ways and intolerant of the weaknesses of men. She'd driven two husbands to their graves and the Rector had neither peace nor comfort with her, though he suffered from her discontent less than others would have done, armoured in his unworldliness.

She returned to the kitchen. It didn't occur to her that some day the Rector, like the Colonel, might not come back at all. Her concern for herself precluded concern for the Rector. When she heard him at last in the hall she didn't experience any feeling of relief.

Her hat and her coat lay ready on the table. She put them on and turned off the kitchen light. She didn't put the light in the hall on. She had a habit of going about in the dark, so accustomed to the house that the dark presented no difficulties. She groped for the handle of the study door and poked her head into the study. The study was dark too, the remnants of the fire in the grate no more than a glimmer, the fire left unmended to indicate her displeasure. She could just make out the Rector's shapeless form in a chair by the side of the hearth.

The housekeeper said, "I can't wait any longer." She added, unwillingly, "It's in the kitchen if you want it," no need to specify further, whether he ate or not immaterial. He didn't reply and he didn't move. She told him, "You know what time I'll be back."

She couldn't tell how it happened and normally it wouldn't have happened. But her fingers slid down the wall by the door and found the light-switch of themselves. The Rector ordered, "Turn it off!"

She said, "Suit yourself." He forgot as the light went out

that she'd ever been there.

At the back of his mind the Canon was dimly aware that he was at home. The legs of his trousers clung damply to his calves. His feet were numb, wet through his worn shoes from walking in the fields. Where he'd been wasn't important to him any more than where he was now. He could think only of the people he'd seen and they were here in the room with him as much as if they'd accompanied him back.

The dull red eye of the fire closed, the fire dying. Todd joined Sergeant Cluff and Anthea Ambler, a third in the disembodied group pressing round the Rector's chair. The Rector wrestled with himself and pleaded with the ghosts by which he was ridden. The cold increased. The house smelt of dust and cobwebs, of meals imperfectly cooked, dank and malodorous.

His thoughts went round and round in his brain. His head bowed and the roundness of his clerical collar cut into his chin. He remembered not so much who he was but what he was, his obligations as a parson to the community he shepherded, the duties of his calling, the teachings of a lifetime. He thought of God, and what was God? Sympathy for errant sinners wrung his heart. He leaned not towards punishment but to mercy, his God love, justice and vengeance not for him. He endured with men and women the tribulations of existence, and men were weak, women weaker, sin original, to be forgiven, the sinner redeemed. But what of the fruits of sin? How could there be redemption unless the fruits of sin were rejected?

He realized the futility of his struggle and he could have saved himself the struggle, but not the struggle, only his doubt as to the result of the struggle. He knew, as he had known all along, that his love for Anthea Ambler, in the final result, wiped out every other consideration. He could keep silent for her but not for Todd, and it had never occurred to him until later that what he was doing would be as much to Todd's benefit as to hers. That day on the road when he swung his binoculars to track the flight of a heron, bringing the river-bank into the line of his vision, he hadn't thought of Todd, only of Anthea. Todd hadn't entered his mind, not then, not until the day of the funeral, with Todd holding her arm in the pew below the pulpit where the Rector fought to eulogize the dead, his legs so rubbery they would scarcely support him, the effort of combining his words into coherence almost beyond his capabilities. Hadn't he paid for his silence as she must have paid for her sin? Had they to go on paying for ever? But what had Todd paid, why should the gift be made to Todd, gratuitously, without anything from Todd in return?

The Canon sat in the Rectory. Anthea Ambler and Todd sat in the Hall. Anthea Ambler said, "I'm frightened," and Todd rang the bell for Betty Metcalfe. Todd told the maid, "Go to bed. We don't want you any more tonight," and Betty tossed her head, independent, unservile, comparing Todd's manner with the Colonel's manner.

Anthea Ambler said, "Cluff," and Todd fidgeted restlessly, forced to a recognition of Cluff, against his will and against his judgment, Cluff beginning to get under his skin too.

Todd said, "What can Cluff do?" and he couldn't understand the effect of Cluff on her any more than he could understand why the Hall and the village seemed alive with Cluff, why the shadow of Cluff blotted out reality and common sense and hard fact.

She asked, "Where are you going?" and Todd couldn't tell her, his purpose too vague, refusing to admit to himself that he had a purpose. He cursed himself for his foolishness and he would have been ashamed to confess his foolishness. He tried to laugh at himself and the effort didn't succeed.

Todd stayed for a while irresolute in the Hall porch, undecided now that he was out where to go in the night. He set off down the drive and he didn't get far before he turned and came back. He went instead along the front of the Hall, by the private path through the gardens into the churchyard. He slunk behind the church in the direction of the Rectory, towards the narrow gate in the wall between the Rectory and the churchyard.

He found himself in the Rectory drive looking up at the Rectory, and the Rectory windows were dark, no sign of life in the Rectory. He took a step or two towards the Rectory door and his blood ran cold. Sergeant Cluff stepped into his path. Sergeant Cluff said, "He's not in."

"How do you know?"

"I've knocked."

They couldn't see each other's face in the dark. Cluff added, "I met him on the road today," telling Todd nothing that Todd didn't know already from his cousin.

"There's nothing to do at night in Egilsby," Todd said.

"You're right."

Todd muttered, "It doesn't matter," and walked down the Rectory drive to the road. Cluff walked beside him. Cluff's dog breathed gently, the sound of its breathing audible in Todd's ears.

Todd turned up the road and the Sergeant turned with

him. They reached the entrance to the Hall grounds. "It's late," Cluff said.

"Are you staying at the inn?"

"Yes."

"Good night," Todd said.

Cluff replied, "Good night."

Her eyes were round and questioning when Todd came into the sitting-room. Her lips framed "Cluff?" and was there no subject of conversation left except Cluff?

Todd nodded. He said, "He was there – outside the Rectory."

"My God!"

"There's no one in."

"There must be!"

"Cluff couldn't get a reply."

"He'd tried?" Anthea Ambler gasped. "He knows!"

"He couldn't know."

"The Rector told him."

"Not yet. Would Cluff have been there if he'd known?"

"It's only putting it off."

Her face turned white as a sheet. She froze, petrified. Her heart stopped. She couldn't breathe. For a moment, before he ran to the French window, Todd was as still as she was.

The rings on which the long curtains hung rattled harshly as Todd tore at the curtains. A hand poised, in the act of scratching the glass with its finger-nails. Todd twisted the catch holding the window closed. He flung the leaves of the window apart and grabbed at the body behind the hand. The leaves of the window slammed. The curtains jerked viciously back into position across the window.

The Rector wore neither hat nor coat. His thin hair straggled over his forehead, plastered by sweat to his skin. His chest heaved. Mud caked his shoes, a trail of mud behind him on the carpet over which Todd had dragged him evidence that he'd blundered into the flower-beds or into the shrubbery. His eyes stared. His limbs shook. Todd let go of him and he tottered, grasping at the back of a chair.

They waited. They waited a lifetime for the Rector to speak. He fought to get his breath back. When the words came they were difficult to interpret. The Rector said, "I heard him. I heard him knocking at the door. It was Cluff. It must have been Cluff." He looked at Anthea Ambler. He looked at Todd. He asked, "Cluff's not here?" and explained pathetically, "I thought Cluff might be here. I didn't dare to come to the door. I listened at the window. I couldn't hear Cluff."

Todd took the Rector by the arm. He led the Rector to a chair, Anthea Ambler moving aside to let them pass. Todd asked, "What has Cluff to do with you? What has Cluff to do with us?"

"You can't—" the Rector moaned.

"I can't what?" Todd exclaimed.

The Rector saw not the room about him or Todd bending over him but the Colonel walking along the river-bank, disappearing from view into the river gorge, a woman crossing the fields behind the Colonel. The Rector watched and the Rector waited and the woman came out of the gorge into the fields but he never saw the Colonel again.

"Not so that you can have all this," the Rector said, his voice high-pitched, Anthea Ambler lumped with the Hall and the estate.

Todd warned, "Quietly! You'll wake Betty."

"For her," the Rector promised, his eyes on Anthea Ambler, "but not for you."

"You talk as if I'd killed the Colonel," Todd said. "I'm only the heir."

"If you had—" the Canon prayed. He said to Anthea Ambler, "I love you. You can't marry Todd—"

They had the same question in both their minds, Todd and Anthea Ambler. If she did marry Todd, if she didn't marry the Rector – what then? How deep was his love? Would it endure for the future as it had endured during this past week? If the Canon had nothing left what would the Canon do?

CHAPTER XI

The legs of Cluff's chair scraped the floor of the dining-room at the inn. He moved quickly out of the inn, leaving his breakfast half-eaten, rushing past Ted Hardacre running from the bar with a duster in his hand.

Cluff shot back the bolts on the inn door. Clive brushed against his leg. Cluff shouted, "Keep the dog here!"

Hardacre recovered, straightening from the wall against which he'd fallen. Hardacre's fingers caught in Clive's collar, pulling at the dog, the dog pulling at him. He could see from the front of the inn Sam Rycroft, in the doorway of the shop at the corner, Sam beginning to race after the Sergeant. Women hurried on cottage paths and clutched white gates. Clive growled in answer to the loud barking of a farm-dog. Other dogs joined in the barking but the noise didn't smother the screams.

Josh Lambert's arms wrapped the Rector's housekeeper. Josh shook her, trying to get sense out of her. Her head wobbled on her neck. The face that peered into Josh's face was vacant as a doll's face. The screams came one after the other through the gaping mouth, the lips unmoving, the screams shrill, blanketing the village. The wind whisked her dishevelled hair. Her hands stabbed Lambert's chest.

The constable released her without warning. He hit her on

the cheek and seized her again as she stumbled. Her screams reduced to a wail. The wail dissolved into tears. Josh's wife appeared and supported her into the police-cottage.

They fell in behind Cluff, men from the barns and the shippons, from the farms on either side of the road. Cluff trailed Lambert. Lambert marched at the head of the procession, in his shirt-sleeves, the neck of his flannel shirt open, without a collar, the waistband of his uniform trousers doubled over the broad leather belt, age-blackened, round his hips. Children on their way to school ran along the edges of the line. The schoolmistress teetered in the school gateway to head the children off, torn between the necessity of keeping the early arrivals herded in the playground and the task of corralling the others.

They crowded up the Rectory drive and Walt Sims was coming along the path from the churchyard to join them. Sims halted near the gable-end of the house. The men in the drive stopped. Cluff looked over Lambert's shoulder, through the open door, into the dim silent hallway. The constable yelled, "Rector! Rector!"

The men behind Cluff took up positions round the porch, quietly, not talking to each other, not wasting words in idle speculation. Lambert didn't move but Cluff did. The Sergeant smelt the smell of the Rectory the closed front door had spared him last night. The living was a rich one, the Rector had money of his own, and if all Anthea Ambler had wanted was the preservation of her standards of existence she could have had it here. The Rectory didn't need to be as it was. There was no cause for it, nothing that Anthea Ambler couldn't have remedied for the Canon, nothing that he hadn't been waiting for her to remedy.

Cluff stuck his head into this room and into that. Each room had its lesser smell as contribution to the overall combination of smells, the sitting-room musty, unventilated, the dining-room stale, the kitchen reminiscent of burnt fat and cold, greasy slops. These rooms didn't interest him much but he stayed for a while in the study, feeling a sense of companionship with the Rector, a sadness because the Rector had strayed, as the Sergeant was so often in danger of doing, from the security of the inanimate to the perils of human relationships.

A blue haze pervaded the study, with its tight-shut windows, a light fog of tobacco smoke shrouding old, ragged furniture, faithful and friendly. Shelves lined the walls of the study from floor to ceiling. Books crammed the shelves, covering every inch of space except the spaces occupied by the fireplace and the windows. Books overflowed on to the seats of the chairs, on to a table, a desk, on to anything that would hold them. In the last resort the flood of books lapped the threadbare carpet, a tide threatening to inundate the room completely. The Sergeant read some of the titles on the spines, the books rare books, divided between the Rector's ornithological researches and his classical studies, Greek and Roman and Hebrew in the original languages.

The bell rang at the school. The morning bus pulled up on the road by the Rectory gate and the driver got down. No one in the Rectory drive looked round. Back in the hall Cluff jerked his head at Lambert. Lambert shifted his weight from one foot to the other, slow in following.

The Sergeant climbed the stairs. His nostrils identified the housekeeper's room on his right. A surplus of books from the study indicated the occupier of the room on his left. Its bed hadn't been slept in but a jacket draped the back of a chair by the bed, a pair of trousers its seat. Articles of underclothing were strewn on the floor. The toe of a shoe peeped from under the bed. A pair of pyjamas hung on the rails at the bed head.

A draught whispered about the Sergeant's ankles on the landing. He gazed meditatively at a door at the end of the landing. He turned his head. Josh Lambert's face poised on a level with the landing floor, the rest of Josh balanced on a tread lower down the staircase. The Sergeant thought that once it started it didn't stop. He wondered how responsible he was for its continuance. Was it better, or worse, to accept the single event, without piling others on top of it?

The Sergeant squared his shoulders. He opened the door at the end of the landing. Fresh cold air from a casement window already open flowed on him and about him.

A pedestal lavatory-pan, its lid raised, the mahogany oval of its seat cracked, stood under the window. A wooden table held a china washbowl with a jug inside it. A cabinet on the wall over the table had a mirror for a door. A high, oblong bath, not boxed in, perched on feet shaped like claws, the taps at its end pot-bellied. The sole concession to this modern age, an electric water-heater, clung half-way to the ceiling in the corner by the bath-taps.

Josh Lambert sucked air into his throat. The bath full, the Rector in the bath. The water pink, not clear, a reddish scum marking the waterline on the sides of the bath. A pink sheen from the water reflected on the chrome arm of the water-heater.

The arm dripped lazily, beads forming at its outlet, swelling slowly, elongating, freeing themselves one by one, falling in a succession of tiny plops.

CHAPTER XII

Cluff said, "He's dead."

He looked down on their faces. The expression on their faces didn't change but a gentleness and a compassion shone in their eyes. Josh Lambert stood in the Rectory doorway behind the Sergeant.

They didn't ask him how. He let them make of it what they would. Out of the corner of his eye Cluff caught a glimpse of the youth he'd noticed on his way up the drive, Sims by himself, detached from the other villagers, on the path across the Rectory gardens to the church.

The Sergeant watched them down the drive. A man spoke. The man said, to his companions in general, "I saw him on the road yesterday as I was coming back from Gunnarshaw. She was with him. She wanted nothing to do with him." In Egilsby "she" meant only one woman, Anthea Ambler at the Hall.

The Sergeant's feet crunched the gravel. Sims stood up to him without flinching. Sims regarded Cluff with an impudent interest, his manner saying for him that he wasn't impressed. He had the measure of the police and he didn't distinguish between Caleb Cluff and Josh Lambert.

Cluff eyed the pimply features, the too-long hair, the drain-pipe trousers and the pointed shoes the youth affected even in his working-clothes. Cluff said, "So now you know."

"What's wrong?"

"If you can't see for yourself you don't need me to tell you." The youth smirked.

"You've had your eyeful," Cluff said. "What are you hanging about for?"

"To see what happens next."

"We don't need you."

"There's no law against it."

"There is here," Cluff said and moved forward.

Sims retreated as if he was going back to the Hall. Josh Lambert remarked, "If he was mine I'd take a strap to him."

"Twenty years ago you'd have done it anyway."

"I'd get the sack for it today."

"Go and put a jacket on," Cluff said. "I'll attend to things."

Lambert replied, "I'm glad you're on the spot. I reckon nothing of this sort of carry-on."

"No more do I."

Josh hitched his trousers: "They've something to talk about in the village now."

"Hadn't they before?"

"Who did you think you were taking in with that tale about fishing?"

Cluff said, "I've as much right as the next man."

"I don't know," Josh said, and he was looking not at the Sergeant but through the Sergeant, into space, thinking aloud. "There wasn't anything wrong you could see wrong, nothing you could put a name to—"

"The Colonel's not the only man you've pulled out of the river in twenty years," Cluff said.

Lambert didn't hear him. Lambert's thoughts drifted, their

incidence altered, their subject Canon Staveley. Lambert said, "She played fast and loose with him. He was entitled to expect he'd get her once the Colonel was out of the way."

"If you want to catch pneumonia—"

Cluff shut himself in the Rectory. He rang up Gunnarshaw. When he'd finished on the telephone he went upstairs again, into the bathroom. He reached to close the casement and stopped in mid-motion. Bottles of pills ranged on top of the wall-cabinet. He looked in the cabinet and found it filled with patent medicines. He held one hand under the catch on the casement window and shook a tin of fine talcum powder over the catch. He blew on the metal and powder erupted in a little white cloud. He couldn't see anything, the smooth metal shining, and he pulled the window to and fastened it. The Rector's dead eyes watched him from the bath.

The Sergeant went to the study. The cold ashes of yesterday's fire hardly hid the bars of the grate. Cluff allowed his hand to dangle over the arm of the Rector's chair and Clive wasn't there. He missed the dog.

CHAPTER XIII

Josh Lambert walked very erect in the road, stately, head up, gaze firmly ahead. The curtains fluttered at the windows of the cottages as they always did. He caught glimpses of movements in the doorways of farm buildings. The road had no pavements. He kept well in the middle of the road, to discourage anyone who might be tempted to accost him.

Mrs Lambert fussed over Canon Staveley's housekeeper. The shock of finding the Rector dead was lessening, minimized by the new importance the housekeeper felt accruing to her. The nervous spasms she affected were exaggerated, the contortions of her face larger than life, her simulated grief out of proportion to her actual feelings.

Josh slammed the door and the tea in the cup the housekeeper was holding slopped into its saucer. His wife shot a warning glance at the constable and he ignored his wife. He said, "How long had he been there?" The housekeeper's face crumpled. Josh told Mrs Lambert, "There's nothing to be done about it. She can reconcile herself to that." He added, for good measure, "He could have been better looked after." The old woman gasped, her eyes blazing. Mrs Lambert rescued the cup and the saucer.

Josh put his tunic on and sat down to lace his boots properly. The housekeeper said, "I thought he was in bed."

Josh tied a knot. "It was Tuesday," the housekeeper pleaded. "My night for my sister's."

"We all know where you are on a Tuesday night."

"He never waited up."

"What had he to wait up for?"

"I did my best—"

"Is he the only one to use the bathroom?"

"If I want a wash I have it in the kitchen."

Josh stood up. He said, "The Rector picked his night." He ate his belated breakfast in silence and left the women to it.

He got to the Rectory gate. He stared at Walt Sims, propping the churchyard wall past the gate. He shouted, "Weren't you told to get out of it?"

Sims grinned: "It's a free country and a public road."

Josh began, "I'll—" and a car, driving fast, approached from the direction of Gunnarshaw. The constable told Sims, "You wait," and stepped into the road, holding up his hand.

In the Rector's study Cluff heard Lambert saying, "He must be about somewhere," and Barker's voice called, "Sergeant!" There were men about Cluff and he opened his eyes, looking straight into the eyes of a busy little man by Barker's side. The little man said, "I didn't expect it to last for ever. It's been too peaceful."

Barker interrupted, "I got a lift with the surgeon. The ambulance is on its way."

The surgeon continued, "We know you by this time, Sergeant. So you've taken to being there when it happens." He asked, "Where is he?"

"In the bath."

"That's tidy."

Cluff told Lambert at the bottom of the stairs, "We don't need you, Josh. Keep a lookout for the ambulance."

The surgeon stood by the bath. He remarked, "It fits in with those books downstairs."

"You'd noticed the books?" Cluff said.

"The old Roman way," the surgeon replied, and bent to test the temperature of the water with his finger. "Is this what you dragged me out for?"

"It's usual."

The surgeon said, "I wish sometimes you and I were in different divisions. What do you want me to say?"

Cluff shrugged.

"I'll tell you he's dead," the surgeon went on. "I'll go so far as to tell you how he died. I stop there where you're concerned."

Cluff pulled the chain attached to the bath-plug. The water slid smoothly away, gurgling in the outlet pipe. A little whirlpool formed over the mouth of the pipe and something scraped on the bottom of the bath, surging in the current as the bath emptied. The Sergeant rolled up a cuff and plunged his hand in. He held out his hand, the blade of a safety razor nestled in his palm. The surgeon pointed to the Rector's wrists, deeply slashed, the skin about the cuts puckered and wrinkled.

Cluff asked Barker, "What are you sniffing for?"

The surgeon put in, before Barker could reply, "He's noticed it too. The air's stale everywhere else in the house—"

"People don't live in their bathrooms," Cluff said.

The surgeon retorted, "They don't often die in them either."

The Rector lay very white in his pink shell, drained of blood. The Sergeant thought of the pigs he'd seen stuck at

Cluff's Head when he was a boy.

The surgeon coughed: "I can imagine worse ways of dying—"

Cluff muttered, "He'd done his share of suffering already."

They'd watched the Rector lifted out of the bath, the Rector carried downstairs on a stretcher, the ambulance driving off. The surgeon paused in the act of getting into his car: "What do you want me to look for?"

"Nothing."

"You're sure?"

"Shouldn't I be?"

"It's a relief," the surgeon said, and glanced at the youth listening by the churchyard wall. "Where's Barker?"

"Never mind him."

"He can always walk back, I suppose. I wouldn't put it past you."

"I've got my car."

"He'd be safer with me, poor chap."

Cluff stopped on the landing. He could see Barker in the bathroom. Barker had the window open. Cluff said, "What are you doing?"

"The sill's wet."

"Leave it. See if you can find his keys."

He looked up from the desk in the study as Barker came in with a key-ring. He said, "There's nothing here."

"No note? No explanation?" Barker asked.

"He wasn't that kind of man."

"But a reason—"

"They know in the village."

The Sergeant gave the keys to Josh Lambert at the front

door. He instructed Josh, "Lock up. You'll have to get hold of his relatives."

"I've never heard of any."

"His bishop then."

Josh said, "The Chapel'll be more pleased about this than the Church."

The Sergeant and Barker came out of the Rectory gate. Barker nodded at Walt Sims: "He's sticking it out to the end."

"There's not much excitement in Egilsby."

Barker objected, "I wouldn't say that. This on top of what happened to Colonel Ambler."

"There's an old saying – things go in threes."

They stood still, waiting for Todd, hurrying down the road towards them. Sims continued to lean comfortably against his wall, an interested spectator, unperturbed by his employer's appearance.

"It can't be true," Todd said, and he didn't fit in with his surroundings, too pale and smooth and slight for Egilsby.

"It's true."

"How?"

"The village always expected when the Colonel died—"

"What?"

"Your cousin and the Rector."

"I wasn't aware—"

"Perhaps the Rector expected it too."

Todd said, "There'll be an inquest?"

"There'll have to be."

"It's unpleasant. This, so soon after her father—" The Sergeant and Barker walked away. Anthea Ambler met Todd in the drive on his way back to the Hall. Todd said, "It's all right. They know why he killed himself." He smiled. "For unrequited love."

"They're blaming me?"

"Of course."

She murmured, "I didn't imagine it was going to be like this."

He looked her up and down. His voice was hard. He said, "You can't go soft on me. You're in this as much as I am." He corrected himself. "More than I am."

He whirled on his heel. He shouted at Walt Sims, "Haven't you any work to do?"

CHAPTER XIV

"Clive," Cluff said. The dog frisked about him in the road. After a while Clive noticed Barker and transferred his attentions from the Sergeant to the constable, but only momentarily, afraid of another separation from Cluff.

They went into the inn and Ted Hardacre told them, "He got away. I had him shut up but he slipped past me."

The Sergeant introduced Barker. Hardacre said, "You must be getting old if they've given you an assistant."

"He's useful sometimes. As near to a Gunnarshaw man as can be for an off-comed-'un."

"It's what we pay rates for," Hardacre said. "We don't get much else for our money but you're good value, Caleb."

"What about some dinner?"

"It's in the oven."

"Enough for two?"

"For you and all the rest of the Force if you want it."

Barker's stomach swelled comfortably. He forgot the Rector in the bath. He felt sleepy and the inn was warm and cosy, the kind of place they dreamed of in the industrial town where Barker had been born, the real thing, not a cheap imitation. The food fitted in with the old oak and the low-beamed ceiling, with the brick fireplaces and the windows split by smooth-sided pillars of stone set high in the walls. He'd eaten until he could eat no more, even under Ted Hardacre's goading and the goading of Ted Hardacre's wife, plain fare but substantial and cooked to a turn. He began to see why Cluff was the man he was if the duties of a detective in the Gunnarshaw division included meals like this one.

The Sergeant collected the final crumbs of his cheese with a fingertip and pushed his plate away. He leaned back in his chair and if Barker felt calm Sergeant Cluff looked calm. His calmness had the appearance of permanency, so ingrained in him that Barker couldn't imagine him differently. He recalled with an effort Cluff's remoteness and uneasiness during the past few weeks and he couldn't believe in their reality.

They moved from the table to chairs by the fire. They had cups of strong tea on the arms of their chairs. Ted Hardacre stood between them on the hearthrug, his stubby legs wide apart. Cluff had a pipe in his mouth and Ted had a pipe. Barker fumbled with the pouch and the pipe he'd bought on his translation from the uniformed branch.

"Whatever he did," Hardacre said, "she drove him to it." And it seemed to Barker that in Egilsby the people didn't condemn out of hand, putting the blame where it really lay.

"If he'd pushed the Colonel in," Hardacre went on, "he'd waited long enough," and there was more of question than of supposition in his words.

"She'd never have married him while her father lived," Hardacre said. "There was a time once, while Dick Ambler was alive, we thought it was all fixed between her and the Rector."

Cluff wasn't to be drawn.

Hardacre said, "She's welcome to what she gets. Whether

Todd's mother was the Colonel's sister or not, he's no
gentleman. He won't be one of the gentry for living at the
Hall, nor for having the estate, nor for changing his name to
Ambler like the Colonel said. He wouldn't have got near the
place if Dick had lived or if there'd been another son besides
Dick. We didn't know his father but it must be his father he
has in him. The Colonel knew what he was about when he
broke with his sister for marrying as she did."

Barker struck a match and his pipe gurgled wetly as he
sucked. More smoke curled from the crusted top of his tobacco
than percolated through the pipe-stem into his mouth.

"Mind you," Hardacre said, "he'll have a tartar on his
hands. She doesn't pull the wool over my eyes, for all she did
for the Colonel." He paused and got no more of a reply than
he had done before. "They'd an old cat at the Hall, blind and
mangy and its teeth gone, that I'll admit—"

Cluff stirred a little and looked into the fire.

Hardacre went on, "—But they'd had it for years, nigh on
twenty. There's something of a man in her. She's not what I'd
call a woman even if she does wear skirts."

"A cat?" Barker said, surprised by the irrelevancy.

"She put it down. She's a hard streak in her. I'm not saying
she didn't get something to do it with, from the chemist or the
vet in Gunnarshaw, but it wasn't a job for a woman. It'd have
made me think twice, I'll tell you."

The innkeeper despaired of comment from Cluff. He went
back to Canon Staveley. "A man can wait so long and no
longer. He did better than most of us would have done. We've
all got a breaking-point."

Hardacre made a final sally: "You put paid to what you

came for, Caleb."

"I put paid to it!" Cluff stretched and climbed to his feet. "What have I done?"

"You're here."

The Sergeant looked at Barker.

Hardacre followed them into the inn passage: "You'll be off back to Gunnarshaw?"

"What did I catch yesterday?"

Cluff got into his Burberry. He picked up his rod from the corner behind the front door, and his stick. He unslung his creel from a hook in the passage wall. He said to Barker, "We'll take a walk. It's pleasant by the river at any time of the year."

Barker thought it was pleasanter by the fire in the inn. Hardacre said suddenly, "By gum—!" and shut his lips tight. He reminded Barker of a wise old owl.

"Ted," Cluff said. He asked, "You've a pair of glasses in the house?"

Hardacre said, "Here, you're not taking a leaf out of the Canon's book? Bird-watching got him nowhere."

"I'll borrow them," Cluff told him.

Barker followed the Sergeant up the river-bank, Clive leading them both. The Sergeant said nothing and Barker couldn't think of anything to say. Hardacre's binoculars weighed heavy in Barker's pocket.

The Sergeant dawdled. It took him a long time to cross the fields immediately behind the Hall. He sent Clive ranging over the fields and Barker couldn't decide why. The river narrowed, flowing out of the gorge Barker hadn't seen before, and Cluff chose a spot this side of the gorge, out in the open. He put his rod together and took a fly from the tin in his creel.

He began to cast. He said to Barker, "Go upstream."

The fly skimmed the surface of the river. The Sergeant ordered, "When you get through the gorge climb back on the top. Keep your eyes on the Hall. You've got the glasses to help you." He looked at his watch. "We'll give them an hour."

Barker trod carefully on the treacherous ribbon of concrete. A suspension bridge, for travellers on foot, crossed the river some distance ahead of him, where a path came out of a wood on a steep slope going up to the road. He started up the grass where the hill the river cut through dropped down again to water-level and there were trees on the top of the hill as well. He worked back through the trees and Cluff was below him, the Sergeant's rod still, the Sergeant's dog watching the Sergeant's line. The constable took out the binoculars and trained them on the Hall. He couldn't see much of the Hall for the trees growing round it and the wall enclosing its grounds hid most of the gardens.

He stayed where he was for as long as he'd been told to stay and for a little longer than that, until it began to get dark. He went back to Cluff by the same way as he'd come. The Sergeant had packed his rod. His creel was open and he had one silver trout inside it. He closed the lid of the creel and told Barker, "I didn't catch it. It gave itself up."

Barker said, "They came as far as the gate in the wall. Todd and a woman with him, looking in this direction."

"You'll just about make it," the Sergeant replied.

They reached the village as a bus drove over the stone bridge. The bus stopped in front of the inn, empty of passengers, none waiting to get in. The driver looked down his nose at Cluff's car still parked on the inn approach.

"You'd better catch it," Cluff said to Barker. "Hurry up. It's the only one back to Gunnarshaw."

CHAPTER XV

"Why shouldn't he be fishing?" Todd asked.

Anthea Ambler returned question for question: "This afternoon?"

Todd's tone sounded less certain than his words. He told her, "There's nothing to worry about. Cluff knows as well as the whole village the reason for the Rector's suicide." He took his cousin's arm. "It couldn't have worked out better. The Rector in love with you, not recently but for years. Cluff in the village when the Rector died." He could feel her trembling. He said, "Cluff's satisfied. Wasn't it clear to anyone, even to Cluff? And if it hadn't been clear who would have chosen a time when Cluff was in the village to attack the Rector?"

He led her away from the gate in the wall behind the Hall, to where she couldn't see Cluff and he couldn't see Cluff. Todd added, confident, "They could never have proved your father's death was more than an accident even if they'd been suspicious – not without the Rector. Can't you understand? If your father was pushed into the river the Rector had cause to do it. The Rector couldn't live with his conscience any more."

She said, "Cluff," and he wanted to forget Cluff but she wouldn't let him forget Cluff. Her obsession with Cluff annoyed him. Sims, leaning on a spade, annoyed him. Sims looked Todd in the eyes as Todd and Anthea Ambler went by him. He plunged the blade of the spade into the soil of a flower-bed but casually, not looking at what he was doing.

Light shone through the windows of the Hall kitchen, Betty Metcalfe's silhouette making a shadow-show in the frame of the window. Todd turned for the back door and his cousin pulled away from him, as if she was afraid of going through the kitchen. He couldn't see why, or what Betty Metcalfe had to do with it, but he followed Anthea Ambler round to the front of the Hall. She walked faster than he did and when he caught up with her she was standing looking up at the façade of the Hall. He said, "There's nothing to keep you in Egilsby."

"You?"

"The estate's not entailed. The will says nothing about not selling it."

Todd called after her, "Why don't you come inside?" and she didn't turn, continuing down the drive. The bus drove past the entrance to the drive as they reached it, the interior of the bus lit. The driver served in a dual capacity, doubling as conductor, not shut off in an enclosed cab from his passengers. They could see the driver plainly, and Barker in a front seat to the driver's left.

Barker had a hand in the pocket of his coat, fingering Hardacre's binoculars which he hadn't remembered to give back to Cluff. He answered the driver's questions with monosyllables, staving off the driver's curiosity, trying to concoct a logical excuse to explain his own return to Gunnarshaw without Cluff. Barker couldn't think of anything except that nothing Cluff did was logical at the time, only afterwards when it was considered as a part of the complete picture.

The driver caught sight of Todd and Anthea Ambler in the Hall drive. Barker looked where the driver was looking. The driver said, "I'd be ashamed to show my face if I was her." His foot bore down on the accelerator. "If they're waiting for me they've had it." The bus rattled and vibrated. "He's tarred with the same brush," the driver added, about Todd. "I wouldn't have either one of them in a bus of mine." The driver spat, "Women—!" and the elaboration of his opinion occupied him for most of the rest of the journey to Gunnarshaw.

Anthea Ambler stared after the bus. She whispered, "He's not going back," forgetting that Cluff had a car if he wanted to use it, and Todd couldn't put up with her any longer, her concern with Cluff a contagion, upsetting him to no purpose, creating a substance he knew was only a shadow.

Todd walked alone on the road, trying not to be glad of the dusk and the lack of street-lamps, with nothing to hide that wasn't hidden beyond the possibility of discovery, unable not to be glad of the protection the increasing darkness gave him. Milking-buckets bumped on the flagged floors in the buildings round the farmyards. The chains tying cattle scraped on the iron rings through which they were threaded. Directly in front of him Sam Rycroft's windows were yellow oblongs in the murk.

He kept close to the side of the road, away from the shop as he rounded the corner, walking slowly, cautiously, and it wasn't the bulk of Cluff's old car that made him falter, but Cluff, Cluff illuminated only vaguely by a light from the inn door, unmistakably Cluff. Cluff faced across the road to the village green, his dog a lesser shape beside him. The moors merged with the sky and the river murmured. Todd moved quickly, as if it had been his intention all the time to go into Rycroft's.

He came out of the shop, cramming the stamps he'd no use for into a pocket of his wallet, and he didn't even glance in the direction of the inn. He found his cousin in the drive where he'd left her and he couldn't get away from his cousin, only to Cluff. He couldn't get away from Cluff, only to his cousin.

The meal Betty Metcalfe served was badly cooked, poorly dished up, Betty surly, her manner off-hand. Anthea Ambler ate little and Todd not much more. He sat afterwards by the fire in the sitting-room, Anthea Ambler across from him, a work-basket on her knees, her hands idle, the silence a torment, what she didn't say worse than what she was restraining herself from saying. He'd had no illusions about her, from the first day they'd met, and, if the reward was high, so was the price. Cluff drove a wedge between them. He couldn't get Cluff out of his mind either. He went over and over the hours that had passed since she'd first told him about Cluff and he couldn't find any flaw, anything for Cluff to get hold of.

The grass reached wetly about Todd's ankles as he crossed the fields behind the Hall towards the stone bridge. The grass grew in tufts and tussocks, the ground, level in the daytime, broken and uneven at night. He stumbled and weaved, straining to distinguish the river-bank, the river loud. The river seemed sometimes nearer and sometimes farther away, never in the same place two steps together. He couldn't gauge the position of the river and he was afraid of walking into the river, of himself in the river, sinking in the river as the Colonel had sunk.

The mass of the bridge loomed suddenly. The gable of the "George and Dragon," solid, windowless, towered on Todd's right. He crept round the corner of the inn, a little forward, unable to believe in Cluff's absence, that Cluff wasn't still there, as Cluff had been earlier in the evening. He could hear voices from the bar and he imagined Cluff's voice amongst the other voices but he couldn't be sure.

Then he was sure, not of Cluff inside the inn but of Cluff outside, of Cluff's hand on his arm. He straightened from the window of the bar and turned, wondering stupidly what had happened to Cluff, where Cluff's fat had shrunk to, how Cluff had become the ghost of his former self. The hand dropped from his arm. The owner of the hand retreated. Todd advanced uncertainly. A voice warned him, "They'll hear me if I shout."

Todd supported himself against the gable. His heart raced. His fingers opened and closed, itching to scrabble in Sims's neck. He listened appalled to Sims's confession, Sims's pride in the hours he'd spent spying on Todd and Anthea Ambler, Sims at the windows of the Hall, peeping through cracks between the curtains, Sims avid for sensation, Sims in search of sexual pleasure at second-hand. He knew before it came what was coming, the nights before last night not the only nights, Sims there last night as well.

He felt sweat cold on his brow. He heard "Cluff" in Sims's sentences and "Cluff" and still "Cluff." His brain wouldn't serve. He couldn't think what to do about Sims, Sims cunning, the inn too near, the inn filled with men, Cluff in the inn. Sims said, "I'm not a fool. It won't do you any good to get rid of me."

Sims added, "There's Betty at the Hall. Maybe I haven't

kept it to myself." Sims told Todd, "Or I might have written it down and left it to be found if anything happens to me." Sims said, "And there's the bottle – what's left of the bottle. Look on the rubbish-dump if you don't believe me."

He couldn't avoid the sentences Sims poured out. He said, "Yes," agreeing with Sims, and moved a little after Sims. He saw Sims vanish into the "George and Dragon" and he knew that when Sims came out it wouldn't be alone, that when Sims walked up the road to the cottage where he lived with his father there would be men about him. If Sims had forgotten anything, or neglected any precautions, Todd couldn't imagine what he'd omitted.

He reached the Hall somehow. He demanded, "What did you do with the bottle?"

"I threw it away," Anthea Ambler said, and Todd groaned.

"To kill a cat!" Todd said. "To kill a cat!"

CHAPTER XVI

Inspector Mole climbed the steps to the door of the police-station, his coat well brushed, the silver insignia on his shoulder gleaming, his cap set squarely in regulation fashion on his head. Barker appeared in the doorway and Barker danced aside, the Inspector with him, each of them in the same direction, trying to pass the other, doing a jig that kept them face to face as if joined by invisible wires. The Inspector had a newspaper under his arm and what Barker could see of the headlines on the page to which the paper was folded screamed of Canon Staveley's suicide. Barker broke the deadlock at last. He pushed by Mole and went off down the street.

The policeman on the desk applied himself to his work. Inspector Mole stalked to the door of Cluff's room and opened it. He glanced at Cluff's chair half-turned from Cluff's table, at a couple of envelopes Barker had opened, the sum total of Cluff's morning mail. The Inspector glared at the duty constable, chafing at his lack of authority over Cluff. He retired to his office to seek solace in his files.

A telephone kiosk tempted Barker and he resisted temptation. He reached the High Street. He'd no dog or stick, his hat was felt instead of tweed, his raincoat cleaner than the Sergeant's Burberry, but he stood, again, in a spot where Cluff would have stood. The owner of a fruit-stall on the setts noticed Barker and remarked to a passer-by, "He's going to turn out another Cluff. If it isn't one of them it's the other."

The morning bus from Egilsby drove down the street. It stopped to eject a single passenger and Barker sidestepped, to get a better view past the fruit-stall.

Sims looked up the street and down the street. He studied the face of the clock in the church tower. A few drops of rain spotted the pavements. Sims slouched lazily towards a transport café and Barker could see him perched on a stool at the counter, leaning forward familiarly, trying to engage the girl behind the counter in conversation.

Todd drove his car on to the setts and got out. Todd looked up the street and down the street and at the church clock, just as Sims had done. In the transport café Sims's cup stopped half-way to Sims's mouth. Todd went into a bank.

Todd put his fountain-pen back into his pocket. The bank cashier riffled the corners of a wad of notes with a fingertip encased in a brown rubber sheath. He pushed the notes at Todd under the grille and Todd, stuffing the money away, turned too quickly for Barker to get out of his way. Barker nodded at him and walked to the counter. The cashier said, "Yes?" without getting any reply from the constable. Barker was looking over his shoulder, his eyes on the door through which Todd had gone. The cashier cleared his throat. "It's all right," Barker managed. "I'm sorry," and went out too.

Todd walked up the street and swung to his right, into a passage beside the Town Hall, obeying an arrow on a notice that read PUBLIC CONVENIENCES. Sims emerged from the transport café, and followed in Todd's footsteps, apparently on a similar errand. Barker stood back against the wall of the bank and waited.

Todd didn't reappear but Sims did, a cocky Sims who passed Barker without seeing him, a Sims who whistled a tune to himself, very cheerfully. Barker allowed him to get a reasonable distance away and then fell in behind.

Barker said, "Just a minute!" The drops of rain had increased to a heavy shower and there was no shelter on the forecourt of the garage. The garage occupied the corner where the High Street joined with roads going west and south out of Gunnarshaw. Barker shrugged the rain off the shoulders of his coat. He asked, "You've got a licence for it?"

A man in a white overall-coat, with a toothbrush moustache, appeared in the wide entrance from which Sims had wheeled the motor-bicycle. The man interrupted, before Sims could speak, "I know better than that. I've given him a cover-note as well."

Sims demanded, "Satisfied?" and swung himself on to the saddle of the machine. He kicked it into life. "You ought to do the Pools too," Sims added. "You look as if a bit extra wouldn't come amiss."

The garage-man said to Barker, "There's nothing up?"

"It must have cost him something."

"You heard what he said."

"He's luckier than I am."

"And me."

"Hire-purchase?"

"Cash down," the man admitted, not too enthusiastically. He justified himself, "I know him. He bought an old bike off me a couple of years back. It was on its last legs then."

"You've got another customer," Barker said.

Todd sat stiffly in the driving-seat of his car, drawn up by the line of petrol-pumps. The attendant unhooked a petrol pipe. Todd said something Barker couldn't catch and the attendant unscrewed the cap on Todd's petrol-tank.

CHAPTER XVII

Betty Metcalfe jumped. Cluff said unconcernedly, "I thought your nerves were in better shape than that."

"You might have knocked."

"I might."

"Or come to the front door."

"They're in?" Cluff asked.

"She is. He's gone off to Gunnarshaw."

"A rift in the lute?" the Sergeant said.

"She can have him."

"So Ted Hardacre said."

"You're not filling your time in."

"Aren't I?"

"I wasn't born yesterday."

"There used to be a cat," the Sergeant said.

"I'm not deaf," Betty Metcalfe objected. "Are you asking me or Sam Rycroft down at the shop?"

"A cat—"

"That's old history."

"They're not so easy to get rid of."

"Who do you want to see, me or her?"

"Did it die by itself?"

"The Colonel rang up the vet. The vet couldn't come. He let her have some chloroform."

"No use arguing with a man of the Colonel's standing," Cluff said, and shot a glance at Clive. The dog's eyes were on the door leading from the kitchen to the front of the Hall. Cluff knew from the dog the door had opened and it could only be one person standing in the doorway. He scarcely bothered to look at Anthea Ambler, murmuring to no one in particular, "Betty didn't let me in. I was inside before she could stop me."

He let his gaze travel slowly round to her and he found it hard to realize that he hadn't actually seen the woman supporting herself with a hand on the jamb of the door since that day in Gunnarshaw a few weeks ago. He compared her now with what she had been then and she had to have changed, she couldn't, by the wildest stretch of his imagination, have remained the same. He spoke to her as if they were alone together, without Betty Metcalfe. He said, "I was your brother's friend. I've known your father all my life. You remember how I came over from Cluff's Head when I was still at school, during the holidays."

She tried to deceive herself about the pity in his eyes and the sadness in his face and she could deny neither. The Sergeant's body went a little slack and he looked suddenly older than his age. He had to prick his ears to catch her meaning. She whispered, "A girl didn't fit in with Dick's interests and yours."

"We were young. It didn't occur to us."

"After all," she said, "I had to take over when Dick died. It didn't matter that I'd nothing to look back on – nor anything to look forward to."

"The Colonel was your father."

"He never allowed me to forget it."

Cluff measured his words: "The Amblers have had a name in the dale since Norman times. I'd do all I could to keep it as it was."

"You're living in the past. People don't care for that sort of thing these days."

"I care."

She said, "My cousin's out. I'm not the man of the house."

"Isn't there anything you have to tell me?"

"You're the policeman."

"Won't you let me forget it either?"

"Nothing will bring my father back."

Her knuckles whitened as she gripped the door-jamb. She laughed. Her laugh pursued him into the open air, round the end of the Hall, down the drive as he hurried to get away from it. He couldn't put another name to the sound she'd made and he wasn't its subject, but it kept up with him, mocking not the Sergeant but herself.

In the road Josh Lambert fell into step with him. "I've been talking to Betty's father," Josh said. "He's not going to let Betty stop."

"They've still got Sims."

"I've not seen Sims about so far today."

"What's happened to the rest of the staff?"

"They wouldn't do for Todd. He's after new blood. They've not done so badly on what the Colonel left them."

"The sooner it's over the better," Cluff said.

Josh Lambert replied, "It won't be over while she's here – and Todd. Egilsby'll never have done with it."

"Can't she see that?"

Cluff drew away from the constable, leaving him behind.

Lambert began to breathe heavily. He abandoned his attempt to keep up with the Sergeant and stopped by the gate of his cottage, accepting without protest Cluff's wish to be rid of him. He put his hand up to his helmet and pushed it to the back of his head, feeling his hand moist with sweat. He leaned on his gate for a while, until his wife called from the cottage, "It's ready when you are."

Josh finished his dinner. He sat in his chair slicing a plug of tobacco, using the palm of his hand as a chopping-block. Water ran from a tap in the scullery and plates rattled. His wife came back into the room with the plates and started to stack them on the dresser. She asked, "Why didn't you bring him in? I'd enough for two."

"There's no use talking to a man in Caleb's frame of mind."

"It's going on too long," his wife said. "Ever since the Colonel died—"

"The village isn't looking to me."

"Can't he stop it?"

"Stop what?"

"Don't try to tell me different. I can feel it as well as you can."

"It's in Caleb's hands not mine."

He poked a spill of paper between the bars of the grate. The bell of the telephone shrilled and Josh dropped his spill. It fell into the hearth, flaring, the flame spreading along its length, leaving a black worm of ash. His wife didn't offer to pick up the phone. He didn't want to answer it but he knew she wouldn't.

"I saw him an hour or so ago," Josh said into the receiver. "Shall I get hold of him for you?" He paused and listened. "If it's that urgent he's likely at the pub." He gave Barker the number of the "George and Dragon." He put the receiver down and returned to his chair. "You're not going out this afternoon?" his wife asked, not needing the confirmation the shaking of his head implied.

Barker depressed the telephone cradle and redialled. He asked Ted Hardacre, "Is he there?"

"Who's that?"

"Barker."

Hardacre said, "Nay, damn it – he's been gone long enough to have got back to Gunnarshaw."

"He's what?"

"I'm not concerned about his bill. The last I saw of him he was getting into that car of his with the dog."

"Didn't he say where to?"

"He didn't come in. I haven't had a word with him since breakfast-time. He's been up the river—"

"Fishing?"

"Not for fish. He set off that way early on but his tackle's still here."

"It's strange—"

"When you've known him as long as I have you won't say that." Ted Hardacre suggested, "Try Lambert."

"I have done."

"He never knows much, doesn't Josh."

"If the Sergeant comes in tell him I've been ringing."

"For what it'll be worth to him."

Barker made a third call and he got no reply from Cluff's cottage. Inspector Mole popped his head into Cluff's room: "You've been busy on the telephone?" He asked, "Have we mislaid the Sergeant again?" and his head disappeared, muttering.

Outside the dark drew in. Barker huddled in the Sergeant's chair, the room cold. The telephone rang and he grabbed it eagerly. The surgeon said, "Tell Cluff I can't swear to anything—"

"Wasn't it suicide?"

"He'll have to make what he likes of it. I'm not sticking my neck out one way or the other. If he wants to have a word with me, off the record—"

"He's not in the station."

"There's no hurry – not if I know Cluff."

The telephone menaced Barker, an enemy. He had the receiver in his hand again and he was wide awake. He gulped and said, "Sir—" He told Superintendent Patterson, at County Headquarters, "The Sergeant discovered him."

Patterson's silence was more eloquent than words. Barker said, "No, sir. There's nothing to add to what's in the newspaper."

"Can I have a word with him?"

Barker sought inspiration in his surroundings and found none.

Superintendent Patterson, his ear to the phone, exclaimed meaningly, "Oh!" He said, "Very well. I suppose you couldn't say what he was doing at Egilsby in the first place?"

"I'm afraid not."

"When you see him he might let me know what's happening."

"Of course."

The duty constable looked into Cluff's room. He said,

"Don't you want the light on?" and put it on to see what Barker was doing. Barker wasn't doing anything, unless thinking was doing something. He kept thinking of Patterson and every time he thought of Patterson he thought of Todd. A second call to Cluff's cottage had no more result than the first. He didn't want to make both himself and Cluff foolish by ringing up Egilsby again. The more he thought of Todd the less he liked what he remembered of Todd. He didn't like Sims at all and Sims got mixed up in his mind with Todd and both of them with Canon Staveley.

Barker went into the outer office. He asked the duty constable, "There's a bus timetable about?" He glanced from the timetable to the clock on the wall. The duty constable bent down to pick the timetable up and then crossed to the main door which Barker had neglected to shut. He looked down the road outside the police-station and Barker wasn't anywhere to be seen.

Barker sprinted, taking a short cut to the High Street. He ran through an entry and through a yard in which lorries were parked, down the side of the Town Hall, past the public lavatories, straight into the middle of the road. The bus jolted to an abrupt stop with a screech of brakes and a car behind it blared angrily, within an ace of collision.

The driver of the bus pulled the handle on the metal bar attached to the door. He said, "I'd be in a proper mess if I'd knocked a bobby down." He closed the door after Barker. "You're getting to be a regular."

CHAPTER XVIII

The bus dropped down from the watershed between the dales. Barker, in the same front seat as yesterday, watched the winding road in the beams of the headlights. He clung to the edge of his seat, uneasy at the driver's nonchalance. The driver allowed the wheel to turn itself and ignored his brakes. Blank walls, apparently built across the road, brought Barker's heart constantly into his mouth. He kept closing his eyes and when the crash didn't materialize he opened them to find the bus still on the road, the right-angled corners and the sharp bends negotiated by a miracle. The driver had a cigarette between his lips. He said, "It's better at night. You can see what's coming by the lights." The narrow road twisted and coiled like a snake. The walls looked very solid and indestructible. The fields on one side fell away into a chasm of darkness. On the other they climbed to the fells, dotted with unseen rocky outcrops and boulders.

"Je-sus-Chr-ist!" the driver said, lengthening the syllables. Barker swayed and put his hand out to the door-bar to stop himself collapsing into the aisle. The bus's nearside wheels jolted on the humpy grass of what meagre verge existed and the bus rocked. It scraped the wall with a grinding of metal that set Barker's teeth on edge and came to a dead stop.

The driver put an arm up to hide his eyes and Barker blinked, dazzled by the light that hurtled round the corner ahead and came straight for them. The windscreen of the bus lit up with a blinding glare. An engine screamed, its whine mounting to crescendo. Barker had a passing glimpse of a figure in the night, lying on its stomach, the saddle of the motor-bicycle it rode far back towards the rear of the machine, the rider bent forward over the petrol-tank, arms outstretched, clutching the wide handlebars, a white patch of face only half-visible. Barker braced himself and the figure angled from the vertical, the motor-bicycle leaning over, flying past between the bus and the offside wall, tyres screaming, flogging the road. It shot away up the hill behind the bus, leaving a dimness contrasting with the brilliance of its headlamp that the lights of the bus succeeded only gradually in overcoming. The bus-driver blew out his breath and the ash of his cigarette disintegrated. He said, "What did I tell you?" and added, "If he doesn't kill himself he'll kill somebody else."

The red tail-light of the bus receded over the bridge at Egilsby, diminishing on the road beyond into a pinpoint and disappearing altogether. The space in front of the "George and Dragon," where Barker had got off, was empty, softened by the glow of the bar window. He could see past the open outer door of the inn through glass in the closed second door and the black shadow must be Ted Hardacre, alerted by the sound of the bus, coming to investigate. Barker strode off towards Rycroft's shop and the windows of the shop were black, the shop closed for the night.

"There's a door at the side," Josh Lambert told Barker from the dark. The constable pointed, "Round there."

Barker knocked. Sam Rycroft studied him, bathed in the

light from Rycroft's living-room. He invited Barker inside with a toss of his head.

"They all do," Sam answered Barker's question. He still had his apron on and he did almost as much trade through the back door after closing time as he did during the day when his shop was more obviously open. "Who doesn't?" Sam asked. He had his head on one side, like an inquisitive bird. He said, "Did you come all the way from Gunnarshaw to find out who does the Pools in Egilsby?"

"It's a quick way to a fortune."

"Not that I've noticed."

"Someone has to win."

"Not in this village."

"How do you know?"

"I'm postmaster and postman both."

Josh Lambert said, as Barker left the shop, "Has he turned up yet?"

"Not yet?"

"You're on your own then?"

"Until the Sergeant gets back."

Josh said, "You'd pass Sims as you came in."

"Was that Sims on the motor-bike?"

"He got back with it this afternoon. He's been roaring round ever since."

Barker moved tentatively towards the "George and Dragon." Lambert told him, "It'll be Shank's pony if you're off to Gunnarshaw tonight."

"I'll wait for Cluff. Hardacre'll put me up."

"There's no hurry. Come round to my place for a bite first."

"It's no trouble?"

They walked up the road in the direction of the police-cottage. Lambert said, "Hello!" and a man with his hand on one of the garden-gates turned quickly. "Mr Todd," Lambert added.

Lambert went on, "You won't find Sims there."

"Who's that with you?"

"Barker. From Gunnarshaw."

"Barker! But the Sergeant's gone?"

"Maybe not for good." Lambert paused. "It is Sims you're looking for?"

"Never mind."

"He'll not be back much before midnight. There's a dance up the dale. He'll be cutting a dash with that new bike of his."

Barker said, "A bike like that costs money."

"Is that what you were prying into when I saw you in Gunnarshaw?" Todd wanted to know.

"He doesn't look to me the type who'd save, however much his wages are."

"It's his business."

"They're not a saving family," Josh said, looking at the unlit cottage. "His father'll be at the 'George.' If the young one's slippery you can always put your hand on the old man."

Barker knew, as soon as he entered the inn, after his supper with the Lamberts, that the men in the inn were expecting him. He stepped into the passage and the conversation in the bar ceased immediately. Ted Hardacre appeared at once and over Ted's shoulder, as he stood in the bar doorway, Sam Rycroft nodded at the other drinkers. Ted said, "I've a room ready for you," and he didn't suggest a meal, aware of what Barker had been doing with his time for the past hour and a half.

Barker said, "I'll go up now."

"There's company in the bar."

Barker shook his head. "I'm tired."

"If you like then."

Hardacre showed him into a bedroom with the bed made up and the covers folded back. Hardacre said, "If Caleb turns up he'll be next door."

Barker sat on the edge of the bed, miserable, wondering, now that he was here, what he was doing, angry with himself for interfering, accusing himself of rashness because he hadn't waited for Cluff in Gunnarshaw, torn between a longing to clear up the relationship between Todd and Sims and a fear that he'd complicate Cluff's plans, if the Sergeant had any. The voices in the bar sounded muted and low-pitched through the boards of the floor and if he was aware of the villagers below him they were aware of him above their heads.

He got up from the bed and looked out of the window, vague shapes dispersing into the darkness. Hardacre shot the bolts on the door. Glasses tinkled distantly, Hardacre setting the bar to right. Barker could hear bottles being shifted on shelves, a fire being poked, lights turned out. The stairs creaked and Hardacre tapped at Barker's door. Hardacre asked softly, "You're all right?" and went on, "He won't be coming now." Barker didn't reply. He took his collar and tie off and undressed to his shirt. He got into bed, prepared for a sleepless night.

Barker jerked up in the bed, the blood pounding in his veins. He couldn't see anything, the room pitch-black, and for a moment he thought he'd been dreaming. Then it came again, a soft knocking, the very softness increasing its urgency. He felt his legs weak as he groped for his trousers, and he was afraid. The knocking continued, endlessly, imperative, threatening.

Hardacre was before him on the landing. Cold struck through the carpet on the stairs at the bare soles of Barker's feet. He walked on the linoleum in the passage as if he was treading on ice. Hardacre fumbled with a chain. He pulled back the bolts and twisted a big key.

The light of the passage bulb fell on Josh Lambert, the shoulders of his cape shining with rain, rain dripping from the brim of his helmet, wet, sticky mud plastering his boots, white-faced, his heavy moustache glistening with rain. Hardacre motioned him inside, into the bar. Hardacre reached for a bottle and glasses from the shelves behind the counter. Barker, with a glass in his hand, neat whisky warm in his stomach, watched Lambert swallow the contents of his glass. Hardacre drank noisily.

The redness began to creep back into Lambert's cheeks. Josh said, "My God, what a bloody mess!"

Barker had a sudden vision of Cluff saying, "Things go in threes."

CHAPTER XIX

"He knew the road," Barker said, the morning grey about him.

Josh Lambert replied, "He'd have taken drink. Drink made him feel a man. They'll find drink in his blood."

A mile or two out of Egilsby, where the descent was steepest, the road bent in the sharpest of all its many corners, dropping from the fells to meet the river-bank, suddenly twisting to follow a lip of ground running parallel with the river. Barker stared at the gap torn in the wall at the outside of the bend, its edges toothed, the stones of the wall scattered in a long, irregular line down the slope of the field on the other side. Bits and pieces of machinery and accessories from Sims's motor-bicycle lay amongst the stones where they had been hurled by the violence of the impact. The gap in the wall, the distance the stones had gone, the parts of the machine broadcast like seed, showed how fast Sims had been coming down from the moors. They'd taken Sims away and a cursory glance revealed no trace of him. If there had been blood the rain had washed it away. Barker didn't feel like investigating more closely than that.

"He should never have got it," Josh said.

What was left of the motor-bicycle had rolled halfway down the slope, farther than the farthest of the stones from the wall.

The front wheel buckled back on itself. The handlebars bent almost in a circle, their jagged ends piercing the torn petrol-tank. Its tyres hung in shreds.

"The one he had before," Lambert continued, "was like a toy beside it."

Barker could see the river and the river had started it but this wasn't the river's doing and, if it was finished now, the river hadn't finished it.

A lorry ground up the lower part of the hill, out of Egilsby, with two men in the cab. Barker stayed on the road. The two men and Lambert climbed through the gap in the wall. They hauled and dragged the shattered remnant of the machine back to the road and loaded it on the floor of the lorry. One of the men got in the back with it. Josh Lambert stood with his hand on the door of the cab.

"You go," Barker said. "I'll walk."

"I don't blame you."

"You got less sleep than I did."

The lorry reversed in a gateway and Barker was alone. Nothing moved in the direction of the village once the lorry had gone. Climbing to the moors the road was equally deserted. A little way round the corner the footpath to the bridge upstream from the gorge branched from the road, following a spur of land before it started down to the river. Trees on either side of the path congregated into a small wood.

Barker imagined movement in the trees. He looked away from the trees and looked back at the trees. An old man approached him from the cover of the trees, taking his time, a sack draped over his shoulders, the patch-pocket on the inside of his jacket bulging. His clear blue eyes held Barker. He made his decision and came faster. He said, "I've been looking for Caleb Cluff."

"I can't help you."

"You're Caleb's man?"

"I suppose so."

Christy said, "They'll be coming to mend the wall."

"It can't stay like that."

"If there's owt to see now there won't be then."

"It's plain enough."

"To Lambert."

"To me too."

A stone on the lower courses remaining at the bottom of the gap rolled under Christy's feet. Barker moved closer to the wall. He watched the old man searching in the grass in the field at the base of the wall, working back towards the village. Christy stooped more. Christy's fingers slid along a length of wire, tracing it to its end. He looked up at Barker and Barker couldn't see that the grass where Christy had stopped was any different from the rest of the grass in the field.

"Sims didn't stand there," Christy said. "There's no stock in this field. I know a hare's form when I see one."

A thought struck Barker. Barker said, "Who told Lambert?"

"I saw Sims's light coming down from the tops. I heard him hit the wall."

"Lambert didn't say—"

"Maybe Lambert didn't know. I made for yon farm. They went to get Lambert up."

Christy twisted the wire between his fingers. "I was closer to the village. I saw two lights, not one."

"A car?"

"The light on the bike and another."

Barker's expression was one of disbelief.

"The bike coming down the hill and then, all at once, a second light, pointing towards him—"

"If there'd been anyone else on the road—"

"Not moving. Not burning for more than a few seconds. But bright, shining right in his eyes as he got to the corner."

"You must be mistaken."

"I'm not blind yet. Look for yourself. He hit the wall full on. He wasn't even trying to get round the bend."

"He was going too fast."

Christy insisted, "The light came on. Bright. In his face."

Barker remembered the bus-driver covering his eyes as Sims drove past them on their way to Egilsby last night.

"A lamp on the wall-top," Christy said. He held out the wire, "And this." He studied the grass at his feet. "A man standing here with a wire in his hand to set the lamp going. Sims thinking if there was a light the light'd be on the road, the corner farther away than it was, the light in Sims's eyes so that he couldn't see the wall and the bend—"

Barker jumped the wall into the field. He said, "There's no lamp here."

"Would there be?"

"But the wire?"

"The lamp wouldn't stay on the wall-top. Once he hit the wall he'd smash the lamp as well as himself. The wire breaking, whoever it was, in the dark—"

"It's too far-fetched—"

But the sharp end of the wire in his pocket, poking through the lining of his jacket and the clothes beneath, pricked

Barker's skin as he hurried along the road, almost running. He tried to tell himself, "Drunk or sober, light or no light, Sims would have known where the corner was," and Todd had seen Barker last night with Lambert, Todd had seen him yesterday morning in Gunnarshaw, at the bank in Gunnarshaw, a wad of notes in Todd's hand, at the garage in Gunnarshaw. Barker remembered Sims outside the Rectory after Canon Staveley had been found, Todd coming down the road from the Hall, Sims continuing to lean against the churchyard wall, the smirk on Sims's face. Barker wondered suddenly whether, if it hadn't been for him, Sims would be still alive. He felt like a murderer.

A girl with a suitcase in her hand came down the drive from the Hall. Barker stopped her and asked, "You work here?"

Betty Metcalfe said, "Not any more."

"I'm—"

"I know who you are. There's not that many strangers in Egilsby."

"Who—?"

"Nobody. They're in the house alone. They might have got Sims to stay but no one else would, not after what she did to the Canon." Betty Metcalfe said, "If that was all she did."

"All?"

"Who's to know whether the Colonel fell in as everybody thought?"

"Is that what they're saying?"

"Why should they put everything on the Canon's shoulders?"

Barker dodged from tree-trunk to tree-trunk along the edge of the drive. The trees ended, leaving him, if he went farther, in view of the windows of the house, across the lawns. The drive continued between the lawns, to the front entrance of the Hall. He watched the windows, unable to see any movement behind the windows. The drive curved away round the end of the house.

A shrubbery on Barker's left helped to conceal the Hall from the road. Barker took to the shrubbery. His shoes sank in the wet earth. He bent double, forcing his way through the tangle, leaves and slender shoots whipping his face. He came to a high wall, fruit-trees trained against it, and turned through ninety degrees, past a greenhouse with pots of plants visible through its glass. Beyond the greenhouse he reached a separate stone building with a high double-leaved door opening on to a flagged yard. The lintel of the door curved in an arch and on the roof above the door the silhouette of a man riding a horse, with a hound at its heels, surmounted a weather-vane.

The door had an iron ring for a handle. In one leaf of the door there was the lesser oblong of a smaller door. Barker twisted the ring without effect, glancing over his shoulder. He couldn't open the smaller door either. The Hall seemed quiet. He hoped the people in the Hall wouldn't be in the servants' quarters.

He crept round the back of the stable, breathing a sigh of relief when the bulk of the building hid him from observation. A round window holed the rear wall high up. He stood on tiptoe, gripping the sill. The stable wasn't a stable any more, but a garage. It held the car Todd had used on his trip to Gunnarshaw and an older car, an old-fashioned limousine, that must have been the Colonel's.

A dust of cobwebs fringed the segments of glass in the window. Barker considered for a while. He felt in his pocket for a handkerchief. He wound the handkerchief round his fist and struck one of the panes a hard blow. The glass shattered. He felt a bolt inside and pulled it back. The whole circle of the window, hinged at its top, swung inwards.

He wriggled through, awkwardly, with just space enough for his body. He had to twist on the sill, folded over the sill with his head out and his legs dangling inside. He let himself drop and it was a long way down. An ankle gave. A sharp stab of pain made him wince.

He stood with his weight thrown on one foot, favouring the other ankle, and the pain ebbed. He stared round the big, bare space. He could see the marks on the wall where the stalls had been removed, the places where the mangers had been fixed. A scarred bench, its top blackened and soaked with oil, flanked him on one side. He turned the wooden peg holding a cupboard under the bench closed. The cupboard door opened by itself and stayed open, the floor under the bench uneven.

He leapt for the window, forgetting his ankle, and the ankle let him down. He gasped, stumbling, his hands flung out to prevent himself from falling, trying to catch the smooth stone under the window. He couldn't find anything to hold on to and he lurched, sideways, the ankle collapsing.

Todd said, "It's loaded."

Barker rolled over. He heaved himself into a sitting position, his injured leg bent at the knee, clutching at his ankle. The ankle felt puffy and swollen, larger than it ought to be. He gritted his teeth and his eyes watered.

Todd reached backwards, pulling the small door in the leaf

of the big door to, the latch of its lock clicking into place. The muzzle of one of Colonel Ambler's sporting rifles pointed unwaveringly at Barker.

Todd's eyes flickered from Barker to the cupboard under the bench. The bulb and the reflector, blooming from the battery case of a big inspection-lamp on a shelf in the cupboard, were smashed, the reflector bent, its shape distorted, the glass gone, the mesh of the wire grid over the glass squashed and squeezed and broken.

CHAPTER XX

Cluff marched away from Josh Lambert, between the farms and cottages of Egilsby, and Barker, twenty-four hours later, hypnotized by the O of Todd's gun, black, gaping, might have saved himself some at least of his agony of mind. Barker didn't believe, as he stared into the throat of the rifle barrel, that Canon Staveley had killed himself. Barker despaired, not for Barker, but because he'd never be able to tell Cluff what he knew. And Cluff, the day before, hadn't believed it either. Barker had believed it then but Cluff had never believed it. The Sergeant saw nothing of the village as he walked. He thought of the Canon and he thought of the Colonel too, and of Anthea Ambler, of his friendship with Anthea Ambler's brother. Respect for the Amblers was strong in Cluff, for what the family had stood for, the link the family had provided with the past that was vanishing into a sterile present and a hopeless future.

The leaves rustled in the trees and the wind blew from the fells. The Sergeant knew she wouldn't come to him, not while Todd was there, not while Todd stayed the realization of her years of longing, not while she called love her want of a man's arms about her, a man's kisses on her lips, her body and a man's together.

He got into his car outside the "George and Dragon," no

hope left that the situation could be adjusted without him, unable to procrastinate any longer. He didn't go through Gunnarshaw. He turned off from the Gunnarshaw road and the dog stirred beside him, recognizing that they were travelling in a direction new to the dog. The Sergeant took one hand from the wheel and patted the dog.

People on the pavement stared at the car. They laughed at the car and at the big man and the dog inside the car. Cloth fluttered where the hood had been torn. The man was alien, the dog alien, both incongruous, out of place in city streets. That the car went at all surprised the city crowds as much as it surprised the Sergeant. Cluff hadn't driven it so far at one fell swoop since he'd rescued the car from a scrap-heap.

He followed the way he'd taken on foot, from the railway station, before he knew the Colonel had drowned. He got out of the main streets, into the back alleys, narrow, deep canyons sided by the cliffs of soot-grimed warehouses. He found again the dingy building, to which he'd been guided by an address in a telephone directory, where Todd had his office, bringing the business he'd inherited from his father to the verge of bankruptcy, piling up his debts by his neglect. The sign that read TODD AND SON. WOOL MERCHANTS was still there, its paint weathered, its lettering scarcely decipherable, and so was the Estate Agent's notice in one of the windows, Todd's creditors, if they hoped for a sale, no nearer a settlement than they had been when Cluff had last seen it.

The Sergeant drove on, by the hotel in a more superior street where he'd gossiped with a waiter about Todd. He crossed the city, not so far as to its present suburbs but to what had once been its suburbs. He stopped the car near an off-licence and if he'd gone inside the shop the proprietor, a garrulous man, would have recognized him and remembered his questions about Todd.

He'd been in the street before but not in the house in the street. He stood on the landing with the stairs behind him and Clive beside him. The woman faced him from the doorway to the flat. He looked seedy and not entirely reputable in his old, stained Burberry and his shapeless, tweed hat with the grouse-feather in its band. His boots had the mud of Egilsby on the welts of their soles and round their heels. She saw him broken-down and defeated. He saw her as he'd imagined her when the proprietor of the off-licence told him about her.

She had hair too fair to be naturally coloured. Her hard features showed traces of the make-up she hadn't recently renewed. Sleep still clogged in white beads in the corners of her eyes. Her housecoat reached to her ankles, the slippers beneath its hem fluffy and furry, the insteps they revealed not quite clean. The coat gaped where it had lost a button.

Whatever he was, whether there were other people in the house or not, he didn't frighten her. He asked, "Mrs Todd?" and said, "He won't be back." Her face hardened more. Her eyes told him he was merely putting into words what she suspected already.

She asked, "Who are you?"

He said, "Not really Mrs Todd. Only for convenience' sake.

"What's your game?"

She didn't take him for a policeman, not for a real policeman, perhaps for a private inquiry agent at the end of his tether. She said, "You've nothing on me."

"You should have made him marry you," the Sergeant said.

"The name means nothing by itself."

"He'll marry me."

"He's not Todd any more."

"What do you mean?"

"He's Ambler now." The Sergeant added, "You're not the only one."

"You're a liar!"

"Do you know where he is?"

"I can find him."

"Todd, or Ambler?"

The Sergeant pushed past her, into the flat, followed by Clive. He caught a hint of fear in her eyes. He said, "They're together. In the same house."

"I didn't ask you in here."

"What did he tell you when he went away on his trips?"

She replied, reluctantly, "He has to travel on business."

"Todd!"

"He'll come back."

Cluff looked round the cluttered room, filled with feminine fripperies, tawdry, untidy, the butts of cigarettes stubbed in its ashtrays, tobacco ash on the floor, bottles and glasses ranged on a sideboard. Cluff said, "He was with you that night, the night Colonel Ambler disappeared. If I looked for them I'd find a dozen people here in the city, and they'd all tell me the same."

"I'm no good at riddles."

"He's inherited enough to keep him in luxury for the rest of his life."

"The—!" and she bit off the word she'd been going to say.

The Sergeant looked at his watch. He said, "It's too late

today. I can't trust the lights on my car."

"After all these years!"

"I'll come back first thing in the morning."

"Save yourself the trouble."

"Be ready," Cluff said. "If it's not the only way you'll find him, it's the quickest."

CHAPTER XXI

They were cramped in Cluff's car, Clive squashed between them. The woman's clothes fitted her too tightly, emphasizing her big hips and her big breasts. The wind tossed her hair, falling to the nape of her neck under a little hat. She hugged her coat about herself. The Sergeant didn't admire Todd's taste but perhaps she'd been different once. He doubted her freedom to marry Todd legally, thinking it certain she'd have been married before she met Todd.

On the hill into Egilsby a labourer paused in his work to watch them pass. The labourer turned from a gap in the roadside wall, a stone in one hand and a chipping-hammer in the other. Cluff braked at the entrance to the Hall drive. The Sergeant said, "It belongs to Todd." Cluff rang the bell at the Hall door. The woman shifted beside him, impatient, and it seemed to them both a long time before they heard feet dragging on the other side of the door. Cluff told Anthea Ambler, "I've brought this woman to see you. She calls herself Mrs Todd."

The woman, her voice filled with contempt, exclaimed, "So you're the one!"

Cluff reached forward and caught Anthea Ambler as she swayed, her face chalk-white, her eyes starting. He held her, stopping her from sliding to the floor. He didn't spare her.

He demanded, brutally, "Couldn't you see what he was? You weren't the first and you wouldn't have been the last." He asked, "What did his promises mean any more to you than to her?" He told Anthea Ambler, "It was the estate he wanted, not you."

He half-carried her, half-supported her, into the sitting-room. She shuddered in an armchair, doubled forward, her hands covering her eyes, her body shaken with sobs.

"Where is he?" Cluff said.

Anthea Ambler didn't reply. The woman who'd come with him in the car didn't move. Cluff got lost in his thoughts, his thoughts confused, regrets mingling with his thoughts, Cluff hating Cluff.

The woman behind him and the woman in front of him grew suddenly tense. The Sergeant came back to the present. His head lifted. He heard it too, tracking the noise to its source, the rumble of men and women collected together, ominous in its cadence, making his hair prick in the nape of his neck. Clive flattened, with his belly to the carpet. Clive's lips drew back from his teeth in a snarl.

Josh Lambert headed them up the drive. It seemed to Cluff, in the Hall porch, that Josh wasn't leading them so much as trying to restrain them, the village left depopulated. Lambert's face creased with relief at the sight of Cluff's car. He ran forward to the Sergeant. Clive growled.

"Barker—" Lambert began.

Cluff cut him short, "Barker?"

"He's been here since yesterday."

"Barker has?"

"Looking for you." Lambert added, "I can't find Barker."

He said, "Betty Metcalfe saw him. In the drive. Coming to the Hall."

Cluff stared over Lambert's head at the people behind Lambert.

"I couldn't stop them," Lambert said. "They've had enough. The Colonel, the Rector, Sims last night, now Barker—"

The Sergeant didn't know about Sims. He hadn't expected Barker to be at Egilsby. He glanced over his shoulder and, strangely, the woman from the city had her arm round Anthea Ambler, consoling her. Cluff looked away, a new disturbance holding his attention and that of the villagers. Christy shoved through the crowd, up to Cluff. Christy muttered, about Sims and about Barker, and Cluff thought he knew now. Anthea Ambler fainted and the woman who'd come with Cluff staggered under her weight.

Lambert mouthed objections and Cluff was shouting. Lambert trailed down the drive carrying Anthea Ambler, dogged by Todd's mistress. The women in the drive separated themselves from the men, obedient to Cluff, following Lambert at a little distance.

In the garage that had been a stable Barker struggled with the ropes round his legs and arms. He bit at the rag in his mouth. He couldn't shout for the rag and he couldn't move for the ropes. Todd came back and Barker's heart leapt, Todd no longer the man he'd been a short time ago, sitting on the running-board of the Colonel's car, sneering at Barker, taunting Barker, before they'd heard a car in the drive and then the sounds of people in the drive.

Todd tugged at the ropes round Barker's legs, his trembling fingers thumbs, the knots resisting his haste. He looked at

Barker's purpling face and removed the gag, his rifle ready. Barker forced back the groans the pain in his ankle brought to his throat. He said, "What did you find out?" and tried to smile, cheered by Todd's blazing eyes, the hate in Todd's face underlined with fear.

Todd urged him to run and he couldn't run, only hobble. Doors banged open and shut in the Hall behind them, men dashing off either way round the Hall, into the Hall, distributing themselves over the house, their feet echoing on wooden flooring on the upper storey. The river roared in front of Todd and Barker, at the far edge of the field they were crossing.

A single voice began to shout and other voices joined in, more distant than the first voice but getting nearer. If Todd shot him Barker couldn't go on, the field blurred by the pain, the pain strangling his breath. Barker fell forward, flat on to his face, the grass wet against his cheeks and lips. He rolled and tried to get up. A little way away Christy came to a halt. Cluff's big form swayed from side to side, Cluff pursued by the villagers, Clive outdistancing Cluff, the dog racing to overtake Christy, passing Christy.

The shot froze them in their tracks, the dog, Cluff, the men behind Cluff. The echoes of the shot reverberated in the valley and the valley became suddenly quiet, only the sound of the river breaking the quiet, not breaking it but making it more perceptible, deeper, tangible. Christy's mouth hung open, his shouts choked back. The answering shouts of the villagers had ceased. Cluff stood like a statue. Cluff's dog, familiar with guns, cringed, motionless.

The rifle barrel swung slowly, inexorably. Barker sat in the grass, feeling as though he was sitting in water. He had his legs extended and he propped himself on his arms from behind.

Sergeant Cluff started to walk forward. He reached Christy. He went by Christy. He reached Clive and said something to Clive as he passed Clive.

Todd called out, "That's far enough."

The rifle barrel completed its arc and reversed, travelling back along the same line, but not for long. The pupils of Barker's eyes swivelled in his eye-sockets, Todd's legs and waist filling the field of his vision, the rest of Todd towering out of view. The muzzle of the rifle pressed against Barker's temple.

Cluff's words carried in the silence. Cluff said, "It's no use. I've been to the city. I've brought her back with me."

The rifle stayed steady against Barker's head, Cluff's statement no news to Todd, Todd creeping into the Hall at the back while he left Barker in the garage, listening outside the sitting-room to the Sergeant and the two women inside it.

"You know why I brought her," Cluff said.

Todd ordered, "Don't move!"

"There's nothing more you can do."

"Tell them to go back to the village," Todd said, loudly so that the villagers could hear him. The rifle kissed Barker's skin caressingly. A man coughed with a dry, nervous cough. His companions stirred, their movement like the trembling of leaves in a breeze.

"I'll shoot," Todd said. "It won't make any difference. Not to me. I can only hang once."

The seconds lengthened into eternity.

"Remember," Todd said, addressing himself exclusively to Cluff, "that if Barker dies you've killed him, not me."

"No," Barker shouted. "No!"

"I almost think," Todd went on, "I'd rather have it that way. You've done this to me. Nothing I can do would make you suffer so much."

"What do you want?"

"I had the Hall," Todd said. "I had the estate. If I had to have Anthea Ambler too I'd enough to last me, to give me the kind of life that's worth living." His finger whitened on the trigger of his gun. "It may be finished for me but I won't let you get away with that."

"It's finished."

"Not yet. When it is finished it'll be finished for both of us."

Ted Hardacre took an abrupt step forward. Barker closed his eyes, wondering whether he'd hear the explosion, if he'd feel the bullet and for how long. Nothing happened. Barker looked again. Sam Rycroft and another man held Hardacre, restraining him, arguing with him. Hardacre relaxed, his strength draining away.

Cluff asked, "Well?"

Barker lay in the grass, exhausted, alone. He squirmed, pulling his body round. Todd had the rifle not at Barker's head but in Cluff's back. They were already a long way away, on the river-bank. Barker watched first Cluff and then Todd disappear into the gorge through which the river flowed.

The villagers were all round him, hands dragging him to his feet. Josh Lambert came from nowhere to take charge and Josh wasn't making any sort of a job of it. They were all talking at once, disputing, suggesting, their voices loud, their ideas puerile. It always came back to Cluff. Little by little the

spate of words dried up. They couldn't solve the problem of
how to get Cluff away from Todd alive, of what to do about
Todd without adding Cluff to the tally of Todd's murders.

CHAPTER XXII

Anthea Ambler came to in the police-cottage. Mrs Lambert bent over her on one side and the woman who'd come with Cluff, on a stool by the couch on which Anthea Ambler lay, bent over her on the other side. The woman smoothed the hair from Anthea Ambler's forehead, her eyes moist.

Todd's cousin thought the cottage door was closing but she'd missed Josh Lambert's return, the phone calls Josh had made, the shotgun Josh had taken with him when he went out again. Even in the cottage, set back from the road, she was aware of the stir in the village. She had a sense of upheaval, of forces at work under the surface, boiling and expanding until they couldn't be much longer confined, of impending earthquake and explosion.

Mrs Lambert said gently, "Barker's been found. Barker's all right," and Anthea Ambler didn't dare to ask about Todd, or about Sergeant Cluff, the vague confusion, the heavy, still atmosphere, as if a natural calamity was going to sweep them all away, speaking more clearly than words.

At Gunnarshaw Inspector Mole listened in astonishment to the receiver of his telephone. He pulled himself together and issued orders in the act of ringing up Patterson at C.I.D. Headquarters. He heard Patterson swear and he hadn't time even to be jealous of the concern in Patterson's voice or to consider whether the Superintendent would have shown the same concern for him. Patterson, forty miles from Gunnarshaw, rushed for his car and set off for Egilsby. Constables at Gunnarshaw piled into police-cars converging on the station, led by Mole. The cars raced up the High Street, their urgency bringing people in the street to a halt. They burnt up the roads, horns blaring, skidding round the corners. Sheep galloped in tight flocks in the pastures. Birds rose screeching from the grass. Hares leapt stone walls in their panic.

By the river Cluff said, "You might just as well get it over with." He felt Todd's uncertainty, the evaporation of Todd's confidence, Todd's plan examined at leisure an empty shell. For a man whose life depended on the speed with which he could escape from Egilsby and bury himself in the anonymity of some community a thousand times larger than Egilsby Todd behaved strangely. Todd's feet slurred on the concrete path in the gorge and the Sergeant stopped, regardless of Todd's rifle. He could sense Todd's brain busy with the difficulties confronting Todd, a fear mounting in Todd, dousing the wild, insane hope that had flared in him like fire. Todd's eyes half-shut and Todd's face contorted. He stared at Cluff, his doubts swelling inside him. His frantic vision of safety so long as he held Cluff hostage dimmed. It puffed apart like a Dead Sea fruit, without substance, its details dust, blown away on the wind.

"Sooner or later," Cluff said, "they'll have to decide I'm not worth it."

The Sergeant went on, "You've no car. If you get to the

road you're only postponing the inevitable. How far is it to the places with which you're familiar?"

The cliffs on either bank of the river pressed in on them. Through the gap in the cliffs, beyond where the fields began again, the thin thread of the footbridge barred the neck of the gorge. The Sergeant scuffed his boots on the slimy, cracked path, askew amongst the rocks. He said, "It started here with the Colonel. The plan was yours, the act as much yours as if you'd done it yourself."

A lethargy, an unaccountable reluctance, imprisoned Todd. The river drummed in their ears, drowning other sounds. Todd allowed time to go on dripping away, tormented with his knowledge of the importance of time, wanting more than anything else to move on, unable to force his body forward.

"Can't you decide," the Sergeant asked, "whether to kill me or take me with you? Haven't I decided for you?" He looked downstream, past Todd, towards where the village was. "They're not coming yet, but they will."

Cluff wondered, "How long?" Time was relative, no means of assessing time in circumstances such as these. A quarter of an hour? Half an hour? Three-quarters? He glanced into the sky, trying to use the sky as a clock. Were they going to stay here for ever?

A spark of life glimmered in Todd's dull eyes. The barrel of the rifle jerked. He couldn't bring himself yet to destroy the one slender chance that remained to him. The strength of his desire to squeeze harder on the trigger racked him with a physical torture, and everything had gone from him but Cluff. Cluff grew and grew in his mind until there was nothing but Cluff.

The Sergeant walked ahead of Todd, Todd not allowing himself to speak in case speech released the springs that confined action. They climbed the footpath that led to the road, amongst the trees, joining the road a little before the spot where Sims had paid the penalty for blackmail. There were men on the road, nearer to the village, inactive but watchful.

The rifle controlled the Sergeant's movements, the rifle the medium of Todd's commands. Unseen, the Sergeant and Todd retraced their steps. The sky began to darken, their delay in the gorge longer than Cluff had thought. The river still roared. Cluff had an impression of the presence of men, men on the road, men everywhere, biding their time, waiting on opportunity.

The village had emptied of men. There were men downriver sneaking through the gorge, Barker limping amongst them, men who'd run back to their homes to grab the shotguns they used in the fields and on the moors in autumn, armed at Josh Lambert's orders. Other men, with other guns, slunk amongst the stunted bushes on the opposite bank of the river. Men moved not only here about Egilsby, men behind Todd, men on this side of Todd and on that, driving him forward, but men on the roads round Egilsby, already on their way towards Todd, closing in on him.

The footbridge across the river led to a hamlet somewhere in the hills, the hamlet hidden in a fold of the hills, perhaps near by, perhaps far away. Todd didn't know: he didn't know there was a hamlet. All he knew was that the path up the river from the village ended where it joined the other path from the road, at the steps to the deck of the bridge, the land in front of him on this bank a jumble of walls and hedges fencing open fields in which cover was lacking.

The obstruction of the gorge lower down spread the river wide, but the bridge had only a single span. Men meeting on its plank deck had to turn sideways to pass each other and, when they did, their bodies rubbed together. Steel wires attached to both ends of the short crosspieces supporting the planks hung from larger, thicker wire ropes suspended between the tops of iron pillars on either bank. These ropes curved towards the centre of the bridge in inverted arcs, the wires holding the deck in place longer at the ends of the bridge, forming barriers as high as a man, but progressively shorter to the middle as the main suspension sagged, in order to keep the deck level. The bridge swung in the wind and it swung more when people were crossing it. Children with the courage could make it swing, if they wanted, through a quarter of a circle, like a long cradle or a hammock slung over the water.

The harder a man trod the more the bridge moved and Cluff was a heavy man. He put out his hands to the side of the bridge to keep his balance and the bridge swung from side to side, more and more the farther he went over it. He swayed with the bridge but more than the sway of the bridge demanded, increasing the swing of the bridge. Todd clung to the wires as best he could with one hand but he had the rifle in the other.

The dog watched under the trees shading the path from the road, where the trees ended and the grass began, and the dog had been there all the time, still in the field behind the Hall until Cluff and Todd went out of sight into the gorge, skulking unnoticed after Barker's rescue. The dog had been on top of the hill above the gorge while Cluff and Todd waited on the path through the gorge. The dog followed them to the road and back again, worming from tree-trunk to tree-trunk, belly rubbing the ground.

Cluff stiffened on the bridge. He didn't know how he knew the dog was there but he knew it all the same. Clive still waited. He waited until the men on the bridge were half-way over before he crossed the grass at a run and jumped the steps to the planking.

The river flowed under the bridge, placid, inarticulate, deep, saving its strength before it swept into the constriction of the gorge and met the obstacle of the rocks. Clive's claws scraped and pattered on the bridge-deck. Cluff heard the sound and so did Todd. Clive sprang for Todd's shoulders and Todd started to turn, too late. Clive's weight knocked him forward and he clutched desperately to prevent himself from overbalancing.

The Sergeant dived, over the side of the bridge halfway between its ends. As the river closed over him he thought the dog and Todd were struggling together and the current, stronger near the bottom, began to pluck at him.

The heavy, dark-green roof above his head splintered under the impact of the dog's gyrating body. The Sergeant imagined a muffled, cracking sound, the water about him parting and coming together again.

The Sergeant hadn't swum for years. The cold knocked the breath out of him. He kicked experimentally and the river forced him under. Cramp began to lock his limbs.

CHAPTER XXIII

The cars from Gunnarshaw, the cycles pedalled by the perspiring constables from the villages about Egilsby Josh Lambert had alerted, came in convoy down the hill from the moor-top. The nearer they got to Egilsby the slower their speed, and if Inspector Mole had little love for Cluff he'd be sorry to see the end of him, the Sergeant at least an interest in Mole's life, a dubious distinction to the police division in which Mole served.

The cars stopped. The village constables dismounted from their bicycles. The Inspector leapt out on to the road, the valley spread below him. The sharp reports, piercing the peace of the countryside, could have only one origin. Round the bend from the direction of Egilsby men raced along the road towards him but branched before they reached him, into the mouth of a path. Across the valley men foreshortened by distance ran on the rim of the land, black dots against a sky not much brighter, disappearing one by one, blotted out, until his eyes focused and he picked them up again against the background of another hill.

The labourer working on the wall swore at Mole as the Inspector scattered the stones newly laid to fill the gap Sims had made. The constables with Mole followed in his wake, demolishing the wall still further. They streamed over the

pasture and forced their way through a second wall, careless
of the damage they caused. They could see the man on the
suspension-bridge plainly, what he was holding, where the
shots were coming from. The country crawled with activity,
men coming up to the bridge on the opposite bank, men from
downstream mingling with the men Mole had seen on the
road, Mole's party dashing down the slopes by the nearest way.

Mole waved his arms, frantically, uselessly, and the blasts
came first, before the words he'd been going to shout, making
the words unnecessary. Flashes from the barrels of the shotguns
lit up the dusk. The shot spattered the river and rang against
the iron of the bridge. The man on the bridge let go the rifle
he was firing and the rifle splashed in the river and sank. Todd
swayed and the bridge swayed. The bridge went on swaying
but the man doubled up, his arms wrapped about his stomach.
Todd toppled sideways on the planking, against the wires.

Mole's lips moved in silent exclamation. He'd stopped
and he started running again. Little plumes of smoke floated
upwards from the villagers' guns. The villagers stared at the
bridge and at what remained of Todd on the bridge. They
refused to look into each other's faces. Mole imagined he
could hear the meeting of the heavy drops falling from the
bridge with the water below.

The thing Mole saw thrashing the river was a dog, the
other thing in the river, waterlogged, sinking, was a hat.
He recognized the dog and he recognized the hat. A young
man limped a few paces to the edge of the bank, throwing
off his jacket. He plunged into the river, fighting the current,
the speed of the current increasing as the river neared the
gorge. Mole and his men, the villagers from Egilsby, pushed

and jostled along the river-bank, panting, pacing the river, tripping and stumbling, catching at each other and letting go.

The dog in the water, and Barker in the water, and now and then, between Barker and the dog, an arm breaking the surface of the water. The river swollen with rain, the rocks needling from its surface, the path along which Mole was fighting his way sinking in a chaos of other rocks, men up to their knees in water, men yelling, men stretching out their arms to seize empty air. Sobs breaking from Mole's throat, the villagers cursing, the police matching their curses—

"Damn Cluff," Mole was repeating. "Damn him! Damn him! What's he doing in there? What's he doing in the river at his age? Hasn't he any more sense than that?"

"I don't want to see her," Cluff said. "I never want to see her again."

He sat by the fire in his cottage outside Gunnarshaw, Jenet on his knees, on top of the blanket wrapped round his legs. A shawl draped his shoulders. He had his feet immersed in steaming water, in an enamel bowl, the water primrose with mustard. His feet showed lobster-red through the pale-yellow scum: hair matted the calves of his white legs below his rolled-up trousers. His nose was the colour of a strawberry, jewelled at the tip with a pearl of moisture, the flesh round his eyes puffed and swollen. He sneezed violently at regular intervals and the cat, irritated, jolted, threw him hostile looks, displeased.

"There's no need," Patterson said. "Not after what she told Mole and Lambert."

Patterson asked, "How did you know about the Colonel?"

"I saw them," Cluff said, more to himself than to Patterson.

"Together in Gunnarshaw. They must have been putting the finishing touches to it then."

"There's little to choose between them."

"It wasn't her fault. Todd—"

"She's as much to blame as Todd."

"What has she had in her life?"

"Her own father!"

"Closest to her, and blindest because he was closest."

Patterson said, "It's always so, but not every daughter takes that way of release. She pushed him in, of course?"

"Todd saw what there was to work on. She believed in Todd. The Colonel didn't matter, the estate didn't matter, nothing mattered to her but Todd. What could she know of men, who'd never known a man?"

"Canon Staveley?" the Superintendent asked.

"They chloroformed him before they put him in the bath. The window was open when I found him. There had to be a reason." Cluff paused. He said, "They did the Canon a favour. He'd seen her on the river-bank, following her father. He'd seen her come back, out of the gorge, without her father."

"Sims knew what they'd done."

"The Canon would never have told what he'd seen. He loved her. But he couldn't have lived with the knowledge."

Annie Croft appeared from the kitchen. She carried a tray. She thrust the tray at Cluff. She said, "Take it. Go on, take it." The Sergeant picked up the glass of hot milk. Annie Croft put the tray down and got a bottle of whisky and a glass from the sideboard cupboard for Patterson.

Patterson sipped his whisky. When Annie had gone he remarked, "She'll have you on your feet in no time."

"If I live through it." The Sergeant held his hot glass gingerly, his fingers tingling. He removed a skin from the milk, delicately, with the tips of the forefinger and the thumb on his other hand. He took a long swallow, burning his throat. He glanced at the door of the living-room and said softly, "Pass the bottle."

"Ought I to?"

"Quickly. Before she comes back."

The Sergeant poured whisky into the milk: "That's better." The walls of his stomach were sore. He remembered lying on the river-bank, soaked inside and out, Mole working on him, spurting water like a fountain each time Mole bore down on him. He thought it would have had to be Mole.

Clive's limbs twitched, the dog asleep on the hearthrug, Clive dreaming, comfortable, glad to be home. Annie Croft reappeared with a kettle. She emptied the kettle over Cluff's feet and Cluff gasped. She eyed Cluff's glass and sniffed suspiciously. She looked at the whisky bottle by Patterson's side and at Patterson. Patterson stared innocently at the beams above his head.

A car drove up the lane outside the cottage and stopped. Cluff wriggled his toes in the water. Inspector Mole, trailed by an unwilling Barker, told them, "I made him come." Cluff nodded at Barker. Barker, red-faced, nodded at the Sergeant.

The Superintendent got up: "It's a long way back."

Cluff said, "You've had a wasted trip."

"I don't think so," Patterson replied.

Mole followed the Inspector into the passage. Barker prepared to hobble after them.

"Barker!" Cluff said. The Sergeant gazed into the fire.

"Stay with me for a bit."

"I'd be glad to."

"I'd like a word with you—"

"It was nothing—"

Patterson and Mole stood by their cars in the lane. Mole said, "I've been talking to Lambert. Cluff knew the Amblers—"

"More than that."

"More?"

"Dick Ambler commanded his battery. He brought Dick Ambler back after an attack. They couldn't save Dick but they patched Cluff's wounds up." Patterson opened the door of his car. "Caleb needn't have joined up. He was getting on and in a reserved occupation."

"He's pig-headed. That wouldn't have been any excuse for him."

"The Amblers fought at Flodden, but so did the Cluffs. They've got the muster-rolls in the church at Egilsby."

In the cottage Cluff took his feet out of the bowl. He left a damp trail on the carpet. He motioned Barker back into his chair.

"I want to ring up my brother at Cluff's Head," the Sergeant said. "It's about a pup for Christy—"

The next Cluff…

More Deaths for Sergeant Cluff

When the police are called to a crime scene at a Gunnarshaw grocer's shop, it looks to be a straightforward case of burglary – but not to Detective-Sergeant Cluff, whose subsequent investigations, following a boy's brutal discovery of a dismembered body on the moors, force him to confront the most gruesome murder he has ever faced.

Cluff calls on his intimate knowledge of the folk of Gunnarshaw to push forward his investigation, but when events escalate and lives are under imminent threat, he must abandon his unorthodox methods in favour of immediate action – which even Inspector Mole must admire – but in doing so, and in his haste to bring the case to a close, he puts himself in great personal danger.

by the same author

Published by The British Library

SERGEANT CLUFF STANDS FIRM
THE METHODS OF SERGEANT CLUFF

Published by Great Northern Books

MORE DEATHS FOR SERGEANT CLUFF
THE BLINDNESS OF SERGEANT CLUFF
SERGEANT CLUFF LAUGHS LAST

www.gnbooks.co.uk